Tiger on the Mountain

(formerly *What Then, Raman?*)

By SHIRLEY L. ARORA

Illustrated by Hans Guggenheim

SCHOLASTIC  BOOK SERVICES

Published by Scholastic Book Services, a division
of Scholastic Magazines, Inc., New York, N. Y.

Tiger on the Mountain

To Dev
who was born in these hills

CHAPTER *ONE*

Munuswamy the schoolmaster drew his big, round gold watch out of his pocket, held it at arm's length, and tilted his head back so that he could look at the dial through the lower half of his glasses. In another two minutes it would be four o'clock. Munuswamy nodded, pleased. After so many years he scarcely needed the watch to tell him that it was time for school to end.

He put the watch away and looked around the room, this time peering through the top part of his glasses. The thirty or more boys of varying sizes sitting cross-legged on the floor were all apparently busy with their studies. Surely the noise was enough, as they recited their lessons aloud, each

1

trying to talk louder than his neighbor so that he could hear himself speak. But wait — there was one silent figure, back in the corner, sitting hunched over something spread on the floor in front of him. Raman, the woodcutter's son — reading as usual, and not his lesson either! Munuswamy frowned and shook his head. He rapped on the desk with the pointing stick that was never out of his hand. The noise in the room stopped, suspended mid-sentence. Everyone, including Raman, sat up straight, eyes on the schoolmaster. Munuswamy waited a full, silent moment. Then he announced carefully, precisely:

"School is dismissed."

Quietly, one by one, the boys rose and filed out. Munuswamy watched their thin, straight backs as they disappeared through the door. Once outside, they would break into a run, whooping across the dusty bit of yard that surrounded the schoolhouse, clambering from foothold to foothold up the short, steep slope to the road above.

"Raman, wait a moment." Munuswamy spoke as the woodcutter's son, last in line, reached the door.

Raman turned. "Sir?"

"Come here." The boy approached uncertainly, his eyes lingering for a moment on the pointing

stick that Munuswamy still held.

"What was it today? Fables? Legends? Poetry?" the schoolmaster demanded.

Raman grinned shamefacedly and ducked his head. "Stories, sir, stories about heroes of ancient India! Just see!" He reached inside his shirt and drew out a small booklet, worn and smudged with dirt.

Munuswamy took the book, ruffled the pages, and shook his head. He handed it back to Raman. "Where did you get it?"

"I bought it myself, from Tumbuswamy the bookseller. With money I saved from festival days." Raman spoke proudly, standing tall and straightening his thin shoulders.

"So you would rather buy books than sweets for the festivals."

"Yes, sir."

Munuswamy peered at the boy sharply through the upper part of his glasses. Raman was the only one of his pupils who came, not from the town, but from one of the outlying farm settlements nestled in the hills beyond the lake. How it had happened that Raman was allowed to attend the school Munuswamy did not know. Usually the farm children were kept too busy at home, or lived too far away to come to the town every day. But Raman had first come a year ago, full of pride and eager to learn, and as the time passed he had become Munuswamy's star pupil, though the schoolmaster took care to conceal that fact.

"Raman," Munuswamy asked suddenly, "how many naiye-paise to one rupee?"

"Why, one hundred of course!" Raman answered, startled. Anyone would know that. It was several months already since the little copper naiye-paise coins had been issued to replace the

4

old anna coins.

"And how many annas equal one rupee?"

"Sixteen," Raman answered readily.

"So then, if someone were to give you naiye-paise in exchange for a one anna coin, how many would he give you?"

Raman gazed at the floor, trying to make the figures appear there as though he were scratching them in the dirt with a stick, as he did when he wrote his lessons. But it would not work. At last he shook his head, eyes still downcast.

"I don't know, sir."

Munuswamy allowed a long moment of silence to follow Raman's answer. Then he spoke slowly. "Raman, you are one of the best readers in the school."

Raman nodded, but without looking up.

"You are also one of the worst in arithmetic."

Raman nodded again.

"Reading is all very well. But —" Munuswamy rapped his stick against the wall, and Raman gave a start "— how will you sell wood when you are grown if you cannot keep accounts? How will you buy in the bazaar if you do not know whether the shopkeeper gives you the correct change?"

5

Raman stood without speaking.

"Tomorrow," Munuswamy the schoolmaster announced, "you will recite, Raman. You will know how to change annas into naiye-paise and naiye-paise back into annas again. If you do not —" He left the sentence unfinished, but the hand that held the pointing stick twitched a little.

Raman swallowed hard, eyes on the stick, and winced at the imagined consequences. "Yes, sir. Good day, sir." He touched one hand to his forehead in a salute of respect and turned to leave, thrusting the little book inside the front of his shirt again. Once outside he broke into a run, fairly leaping across the yard and up the little slope to the road. He did not look back, and he did not see Munuswamy the schoolmaster step to the doorway to watch him, the pointing stick still in his hand and a smile lifting the corners of his thin lips.

The other boys had already disappeared, but Raman cared little, for he did not seek their company. A year ago, when Raman had first come to the school, the others had asked him each day to join them in their afterschool play down by the lake. Raman had always refused, anxious to get home in time to finish his chores and still have some daylight left in which to study. As time went on, the other boys no longer bothered to ask. Later Raman had sometimes wished they would, for he was too shy to join them without an invitation. But today it did not matter. Today he had the book. He could feel it jiggling against his body as he scaled the slope in great leaps.

Raman hurried along the schoolhouse road until it merged with the steep bazaar street. Up the street he turned, but long before he reached the top he had stopped running and was walking slowly and breathing heavily. When at last he came to level ground, he squatted down beside the road to rest, rubbing his nose with his hand because the cold air he had gulped in while running had made it tickle.

The afternoon was chilly indeed, and clouds rising in the southwest promised rain during the night. Far above Raman's head the wind sighed through the long gray leaves of the blue gum trees. Long shadows stretched across the road, crowding out the pale warmth of the late afternoon sunshine.

As he rested, Raman tried reciting under his breath: "One hundred naiye-paise make one

7

rupee. Sixteen annas make one rupee. Twenty-five naiye-paise make one quarter of a rupee. Four annas make one quarter of a rupee. And so one anna equals —" He broke off, scowling. How complicated it all was! The new money was supposed to be easier, but learning to change from the old to the new was hard indeed.

Raman picked up a twig and drew twenty-five little marks on the ground. Then he tried dividing them up into four equal groups. But there was an extra mark left over, and he did not know what to do with it. He threw the stick down in disgust and sat back on his heels.

A bullock cart rumbled past and headed down the hill, with the grating shriek of wooden brake against rough wooden wheels. Raman waved to the driver, who returned the greeting. He rose then and continued on up the street, keeping just off the edge of the sidewalk because the dusty ground felt better to his bare feet than did the cold concrete pavement.

Over on the other side of the road the last of the vegetable sellers was slowly putting away in her basket the few bunches of carrots and beets that had not been sold that day. She caught sight of Raman and called out, "Your mother has gone

8

home. She sold all her vegetables by noontime, she was that lucky."

Raman nodded and waved in reply as he passed. There would be a good dinner tonight if all the vegetables had been sold. Plenty of rice, and probably some curry or pepper water to go with it. He was hungry. But still, there was no need to hurry home. His father would not have returned yet, and no one would eat before his father came home.

Raman had left the bazaar behind now, with its jumble of voices and its smell of hot oil and frying spices. The road still climbed, but less steeply. There was no longer any sidewalk, and smooth black pavement had replaced the uneven cobblestones of the bazaar hill. At one point where the road curved widely Raman paused, looking down over the green slopes to the right, over the sprinkling of red tile roofs to the gleam of lake water nearly hidden by trees. Faint voices rose from below, punctuated by shrieks of laughter. Raman could not see the owners of the voices, but he could guess who they were: Salwari and Muttu and the other boys from the school, gone down to look for frogs in the reedy waters of the lake. Raman turned his back on the voices and followed the road up the hill.

Almost at the crest of the hill a path led off to the left. Raman turned aside and followed it. It was a narrow path, covered with thick dust that pressed up between Raman's bare toes. The hill people called this the "path on the edge of the mountain," and rightly so, for it was cut right out of the rock itself. From its edge the lonely slopes dropped down, down, without a pause, until they merged with the misty, glittering patchwork of the South Indian plains. As far as one could see, the plains stretched out, patterned with squares of red plowed earth and brilliant green rice fields and blue ponds left by the rains. Puffs of clouds hung suspended between the plains and the path on which Raman stood, so that he could look down on them and see the dark shadows they cast on the land below.

Raman wondered, as he always did, what it must be like to live in one of the Merkin bungalows that perched on the crest of the hill just above the path on the edge of the mountain. From the windows one could watch the plains all day long, from the time of earliest sunlight to the last tinge of sunset, and then on into the night when the darkness below the cliff was sparked with the pale clustered lights of the plains villages and the brighter jewels that marked the location of the larger towns. How he envied the Merkin people who could live in such bungalows! Yet for most of the year the bungalows were empty, with doors padlocked and windows shuttered. It was only during the "hill season," the two or three months between the northeast and the southwest monsoons, that the Merkin people left their homes and schools and missions on the plains and came to the hills to escape the heat.

The Merkin people had come to India from a land far across the Black Waters, and Munuswamy the schoolmaster called it, in his careful, precise way, "America." But to Raman and to the other hill folk, those strange, pale people with the funny, flat, slow voices were the "Merkins," and the season when they came to the hills was the best of the year, for then there were jobs for everyone, and no one went hungry. Raman's mother sold all her vegetables every day, and his father sold many bullock carts of firewood, and Raman himself and his sister Vasanti found a ready market for all the mushrooms they could gather and for the bags of pine cones that were used as kindling. Now, Raman knew, the monsoon rains had begun, ending the hot season, and already most of the Merkin people had left the hills and returned to the plains. Few of the bungalows were still occupied, and even those were sure to be empty before long.

Raman had come to a sharp curve in the path, where a rocky ledge jutted out of the cliff above. The cliff itself was a little less steep here, and there were toeholds here and there where hardy plants clung, or where part of the rock had weathered away, leaving a little hollow gouged out of the surface. Raman left the path and started up the face of the cliff, climbing carefully from one toehold to the next. In a moment he had reached the ledge, which was just wide enough for him to sit on. With a sigh he dropped down, leaning back against the cliff, and closed his eyes. The next instant he opened them again. There was still time. The sun was already low. He reached inside his shirt for the little booklet, hunched himself into a more comfortable position, and took up the story again where he had left off when Munuswamy the schoolmaster had rapped on the table with his pointing stick.

CHAPTER  *TWO*

The horizon was already slicing off a bit of the sun when Raman turned the last page of the book and with a sigh straightened up and blinked his eyes at the hazy expanse of plain below him. The rain ponds were tinted red-gold now, and the cottony clouds also. Deepening shadows were creeping up the slopes far to his left, out of reach of the sun's last rays. Raman allowed himself to sit a moment, eyes squinted together so that the neatly marked out red and green patches below seemed to swim together. It was on a plain like this one that the battle had taken place, the battle he had just read about. Armies of warriors mounted on elephants or horses, or riding in swift chariots, had charged across the plain to the sound of drums and trumpets and conch shells blowing. Arrows had filled the air, as thick as a swarm of locusts, and in the midst of the battle Arjuna and Bhishma, the two greatest warriors, had fought each other from chariots pulled by snow-white horses.

Sandaled footsteps along the path below roused Raman from his thoughts. He peered over the ledge and caught sight of his own father coming around the curve of the path. Raman called out to him, and saw his father stop short in surprise. Stuffing the book inside his shirt again, Raman clambered down to the path.

"Raman, what are you doing here?"

"I stopped a while to rest and —"

"— and to read." His father finished the sentence for him. "Whenever you buy one of those books —!" He shook his head, but there was no anger in his voice, and he did not try to conceal the pride in his eyes as he looked at his son. He walked on, and Raman fell into step beside him.

"I was just thinking that those plains down there are like the ones in the book, where the battle took place," Raman confided.

He paused, waiting for his father to ask "What

battle?" so that he could tell him all about it. But instead his father merely nodded. "You have been reading about Krishna and Arjuna and Bhishma."

"You know about them?" Raman's eyes widened in surprise. "But you don't —" He broke off and looked away quickly, embarrassed.

"I don't know how to read?" His father's tone was light, but with a slight edge of bitterness. "Do not think, my son, that all knowledge must come from books. I learned those stories when I was younger than you."

"How?" Raman asked curiously.

"From my father, who learned them from his father."

"But you never told them to me."

"I am not a storyteller, and then too I always hoped that someday you would go to school and learn to read them for yourself."

"But Appa, your father and his father also — they did not read."

"No — you are the first in the family who has learned to read, the first who has gone to school. You are very lucky, Raman. I learned only what my father could tell me, and he learned only what his father could tell him, but you — you can learn many things that none of us has ever known. Not just stories, but many, many other things."

Raman drew a deep breath, his dark eyes glowing. That was what he wanted: to learn many, many things! He would not be just a woodcutter's son. He would not become just a woodcutter when he grew up. He would be more: a man who read books, a scholar.

Raman gazed out over the plains again. Across the middle of the wide expanse, barely visible through the haze, there crept a small insect, like the little centipedes that lived under the rocks along the road, but with a whiff of smoke trailing along behind it. Raman stopped short. "Look, Appa, a train!"

Raman's father stopped also. "The train to the city," he nodded.

"Tell me about it," Raman urged. "How big is it, really, Appa?" He knew the answer by heart, but he never tired of hearing it.

"Each carriage is bigger than the bus that comes up here from the plains," his father answered as he always did. "The engine is bigger still, and has fire inside it that makes the wheels turn so that it can pull the carriages behind it."

"If only the train could come up here to the hills!"

"No one could build a track up these steep slopes. It took many, many years to build the road so that the bus could travel up and down. Before that, the only way was to come on foot."

"I have heard Tata Natesan tell of those days," Raman said as they walked on again. "Appa, when will I be able to go down to the plains myself?"

"It will be a long time, my son. And do not be too anxious. You might not find it so wonderful. For one thing, it is very hot indeed."

Raman wondered what "hot" would be like, but he could not even imagine it. Never in his twelve years had he left the cool mountain slopes where he was born. Here the sun was strong, but the air was never really hot. The nights were always chill and damp, and days would go by when the sun did not shine at all. Then the swollen clouds brought heavy monsoon rains, and cold winds whipped the trees about breaking off huge branches and flinging them to the ground, and churned the lake waters to froth that piled up against the banks.

But heat or no heat, Raman thought, eyes on the blurred horizon beyond which the city lay, he would go there someday, down to that distant, glittering world. For it was there that a scholar belonged. Who ever heard of a real scholar living in these hills?

They had reached the point where the path on the edge of the mountain came out onto the road again. They walked in silence now, except for the slap-slapping of Raman's father's sandals on the pavement. It was twilight, and Raman shivered slightly in his thin shirt and tattered shorts. The wind had the breath of rain upon it.

There at last was their house, nestled in a level space along the side of a shallow ravine. The mud-brick walls and the thatched roof still seemed to hold some of the warmth of sunset glow. All around the house were the neat plots of vegetables grown for the market—rows of feather-leaved carrots, a few stalks of straggling corn; round, leafy cabbages in one section, dark-red beet tops in another; a thickly planted plot of spinach, dull and dark in contrast to the bright-green leaf lettuce beside it; in the background, a rough framework that held a sprawling grapevine. Below the house ran a thin, shallow stream, where some of the neighbor children were still splashing, shrieking at the coldness of the water, in their evening bath.

Raman's seven-year-old sister Vasanti sat on the doorstep, her small dark head bent in concentration over the work she held in her lap.

"Thangachi, there is no light. How can you sew still?" Raman called to her as they approached.

Vasanti stood up with a sigh. "I've just finished. See, I've mended our blanket." She held out her work so that Raman could see the big, awkward stitches that drew together the holes in the woolen cloth. "While we were asleep last night, Dasan put his foot through the biggest hole again and tore it even more."

"I didn't mean to," protested five-year-old Dasan, coming around the corner of the house just as Vasanti spoke. He carried an armload of small sticks gathered from the ravine.

"Of course not. You must have been jumping in your dreams, Thambi." Vasanti smiled and reached out to tug at Dasan's short, curly hair as he slipped past her into the house. The children rarely used each other's names. To Raman, Vasanti was Thangachi, or "Little Sister," and she in turn called him Enna, or "Elder Brother." Dasan was Thambi, "Little Brother," to them both.

Vasanti folded the blanket carefully and went inside to tuck it away in a corner until nightfall. Raman and his father followed her into the dim room. A pot of rice was boiling over the small fire on the corner hearth. Raman's mother squatted in front of the fire, stirring the rice, and she took the sticks Dasan had brought and poked them into the flames. Over in another corner of the room, the baby lay wrapped in a blanket, chuckling to himself.

"The rice is nearly done," Raman's mother said, looking up as they came in. "You have just time to wash, and it will be ready."

It was hard for Raman to leave the smoky warmth of the room and go out again into the chilly evening, and harder still to splash the cold stream water onto his face and neck and over his arms and bare legs. The neighbor children had gone to their own houses, and Raman and his father were alone. Clouds had made the darkness fall swiftly, and the damp air was filled with the voices of frogs and night insects.

When they returned to the house, Vasanti was helping her mother spread out the banana leaves on the floor. Then her mother piled hot, steaming rice onto each leaf — first for Raman's father, and for Raman and Dasan, and lastly for Vasanti and herself. A little rice she set aside and mixed with water for the baby. There was pepper water too — a hot soup of green chilies to mix with the rice to give it flavor. Raman scooped up the hot rice in his fingers, tossing it about gently until it was cool enough to transfer to his mouth, and sucked his breath in and out to soothe the hot sting of the chilies.

No one spoke during the meal. The fire on the hearth sputtered and died down without more sticks to feed it, and there was no oil for the lamp to bring light to the dark room. When the meal was finished, Vasanti gathered up the leaves and burned them, and Raman's mother took the brass rice pot outside to scrub with sand and ash until its smoke-stained sides gleamed anew. She fed the baby his rice and wrapped him up to sleep, and then came outside again to grind the rice and dal for the *dosais* the next morning. The rice and the dal, which was like dried white peas split in half, had been soaking for several hours, and now she put them into the hollow of the grinding stone and turned the heavy stone pestle around and around inside the hollow until the rice and the dal were ground to a thick paste, ready to be left overnight and then fried the next morning into the lacy-thin cakes called *dosais*.

Vasanti and Dasan had already spread out the woven palm-leaf mat they slept on and covered themselves with the mended blanket ready for sleep. Raman sat quietly in front of the house, leaning his back against the rough wall, and scratched some words in the dust with a twig. Remembering the schoolmaster's warning, he erased the words and drew some numbers instead. Then he erased those and drew twenty-five little lines to represent the twenty-five naiye-paise that would equal a four-anna piece. He divided them into four groups of six lines each, and gazed frowning at the one line that was left over. You couldn't divide a naiya-paisa into four parts. Four annas,

twenty-five naiye-paise; one anna, six naiye-paise he decided. If anyone wanted to argue about the extra one fourth of a naiya-paisa . . . well then, let him argue. He hoped Munuswamy the schoolmaster would agree.

"There is rice for two days left." Raman's mother spoke from her place at the grinding stone. It was almost as though she spoke to no one in particular. Raman's father did not answer. He squatted on the doorstep, looking out across the vegetable fields into the darkness that hid the stream and the pine grove beyond.

"Today I sold all the vegetables to a Merkin lady who was going down on the bus," Raman's mother went on. "Tomorrow it will not be so easy. Many of the women took half their vegetables home with them today, unable to sell them."

Raman's father remained silent for some minutes more. At last he sighed and spoke. "Tomorrow I shall go down to the plains."

Raman heard the sadness in his father's voice and winced at the thought of the months ahead. Each year when the season had ended and the Merkin people had left, many of the hillmen went down to the plains to seek work in the towns and larger villages there. Their families stayed in the hills, living as best they could until the men could send money up to them. If the men found work, well and good; if jobs were scarce on the plains as well . . .

"This year Raman is of an age to help more," his mother was saying. "Last Saturday he and Vasanti sold berries for fifteen annas."

"He is a good boy," his father answered quietly. Raman felt the warmth creep over him. His father spoke little; it was his way. To know that his father thought well of him was good indeed.

"There are many things we need beside food," his mother sighed. "Clothes for the baby and for Dasan, blankets, a new water vessel . . ."

"And a sari for you," Raman's father interrupted. "I know well how many things there are. There is no end to them. It is settled; I will go tomorrow. By next week perhaps I can send you enough for the food, and maybe for some clothing as well. In the meantime —" he hesitated, then went on quietly "— in the meantime Raman can help. He will have to leave school, of course."

Raman straightened up, opening his mouth to protest, but he bit the words back instead. Something in his father's voice stopped him. He slumped back against the wall.

Raman's mother finished her grinding and put the rice-and-dal paste in a covered vessel to stand until morning. She rose to go into the house and caught sight of Raman.

"Eh, Raman, time to be asleep. Tomorrow we rise early to pick the vegetables before the bus leaves."

Raman scrambled to his feet, staggering a little because one foot had fallen asleep. He walked numbly into the house, groped in the darkness for his own palm mat, and unrolled it on the floor. The shirt and shorts that he wore were his only clothes, and so he had none to change into. He lay down on the mat and wrapped himself in his blanket.

His parents came in too, and his mother picked up the baby, who whimpered slightly, and wrapped him close within her own blanket before she lay down to sleep. The first drops of night rain fell on the roof, then a few more, then faster and faster until the night was full of sound. Raman pulled his blanket closer around him and over his face. It seemed a long time until sleep came.

CHAPTER **THREE**

Before the sun's rays had reached into the ravine where their house stood, the children were up and gathering the vegetables to be taken to the town. Raman and Dasan tugged the beets and carrots out of the damp earth, and Vasanti counted them into bunches of six and tied them with long pieces of tough, dry grass. Then Dasan chose the largest clumps of lettuce and the fullest cabbages, and Raman looked among the cornstalks for the ripe ears and pulled up enough spinach to make half a dozen bunches. Together the children packed the vegetables lightly into the huge basket that their mother would carry on her head when she walked into town. By the time they had finished their mother had fried the *dosais* and ground the chili-hot coconut paste to eat with them, and their father had packed his few belongings into the small tin box that he would take with him down to the plains.

When breakfast was over, the whole family set out for the bazaar. Raman's father strode ahead, with Raman at his side carrying the tin box. Raman's mother followed, the vegetable basket balanced gracefully on her head. Vasanti walked beside her, carrying the baby on one hip and leading Dasan by the hand. For a time no one spoke. They passed a few others on their way to town: fagot vendors trotting along with piles of six-foot-long sticks on their heads, two small boys guiding a herd of gray buffaloes down to the lakeside to graze, other women with baskets of vegetables.

"Look, a *roly-puchi!*" Dasan, who had broken away from Vasanti once they were on the paved road, ran ahead and held out his hand to Raman, revealing in his palm the queer black insect that, when touched, rolled itself up into a tight scaly ball the size of a large marble. Any other day Raman would have grinned with delight and joined in a hunt for more, but today he merely nodded and walked on.

Lucky Dasan! For him nothing would change when their father was gone. He would romp about the ravine and the pine groves, laughing and playing as always, with little to do for the household except to gather a few kindling sticks when they were needed or pull a few vegetables in the mornings. He was too young to go to school, and perhaps anyway he did not care.

"But I care," Raman thought bitterly, "and I have to be the one to give it all up."

He remembered the wonderful singing pride he had felt the year before when his father had first announced the plan to send Raman to school. He thought of the growing excitement of each day, as the little circles and lines and curves of Tamil script came to mean sounds and then words, and he, Raman, the woodcutter's son, had become the first in his family — the first even in his village — who had learned to read.

Last year had been a good year. There had been money saved to buy food while Raman's father looked for a job on the plains, and then there had been money arriving each week, so that they need not worry about the rice supply for the days ahead. This year it was different. Everything had gone wrong. Insects had destroyed many of the vegetables before they could be marketed. Then, in mid-season, one of the wooden wheels on his father's firewood cart had split. Replacing it had taken time, and without the cart there was no way to haul wood from the forest where it was cut. To make matters worse, the monsoon rains had come earlier than usual, ending the hill season before the expected time. When the Merkin people, who bought the heavy logs for the fireplaces of their bungalows, had gone, there was no market for the wood Raman's father cut, for the hill people had only small cooking hearths that used kindling and light sticks they gathered themselves or bought from the fagot vendors.

And as though all that were not enough, there was the new baby too, needing rice now, and buffalo milk besides. Raman turned his thoughts away abruptly, ashamed of the resentment he felt. As though the baby were to blame!

They had reached the top of the bazaar street. Raman's mother went to take her place with the other women who lined up in a row by the side of the road. Carefully she lifted out the vegetables and set them neatly on the ground in front of her. Wet with the rain, they made a colorful picture. On other days Raman would have stayed to help her, glancing out of the corner of his eye at the vegetables the other women had brought, to see if any had beets or carrots as big as theirs, or spinach or lettuce so crisp and freshly picked. To-day the children continued on down the bazaar street toward the bus stand with their father. Their mother remained behind, keeping the baby with her. She must stay with the vegetables, and could only wave as the bus went by along the road.

The bus was already parked in front of the bus stand, its blue and red sides shiny from the rain of the night before. Two men were on the roof of the bus, stowing away the baskets and boxes that the other workmen below tossed up to them, and then tying the whole load down with ropes and covering it with canvas in case there should be rain on the downward journey. The bus was crowded, for a great many hill folk were going down, as Raman's father was, to find work on the plains. There were a few Merkin people, too, who had stayed up in the hills longer than the rest.

"Vasanti, go and buy a sweet for yourself and one for Dasan." Their father pressed a small coin into Vasanti's hand. The two younger children ran off, laughing with pleasure. Raman stayed quietly behind.

31

"Raman, there is a coin for you also, but I suppose you will not want to buy sweets with it." Raman's father looked down at his eldest son, a touch of teasing in his voice. Raman shook his head. His father knew as well as he that the coin would be kept until others had joined it, until there were enough to buy yet another book from Tumbuswamy the bookseller.

Raman's father was silent a moment. Then he spoke soberly. "I am sorry about your schooling, Raman. I know how much it means to you. Perhaps after I have found a job and have been able to send some money . . ." He left the sentence unfinished.

"He does not want to promise," Raman thought. "But he does know how I feel." A sudden rush of gratitude warmed him.

"In the meantime," his father went on slowly, "we shall do this: for every rupee that you earn for the household, you shall have one naiya-paisa to keep for yourself."

Raman's eyes widened with astonishment and pleasure. His father smiled. "I have talked with your mother also, and she . . . has agreed." He hesitated a moment. His voice dropped lower. "She perhaps does not understand quite so well

that it is important to dream as well as to work. When I was your age, I too dreamed of becoming more than a woodcutter like my father before me. That is why I wanted you to go to school when you were old enough, so that for you it might become more than just a dream."

"Appa, it is not that I would be ashamed to be a woodcutter —" Raman began quickly.

"Of course not. Nor am I ashamed. But keep your dream, Raman. Hold onto it with all your strength. Who knows what is ahead for you?" He raised his voice again. "Take care, now. You are responsible for the others. In my absence you are head of the household and, for the time being, the chief wage earner. I leave everything with you."

Vasanti and Dasan had returned, hands sticky and faces smiling. Raman's father lifted them each in turn for a last farewell. The ticket seller came out of his dingy office to ring the warning bell, striking with an iron bar the big iron triangle that hung from a pole beside the bus stand. Raman's father stepped up into the bus and made his way toward the back, where there was still a place left near the window. The bus driver, already in his seat, reached out the window and squeezed the rubber bulb of his horn. While the hoarse squawk of the horn still echoed from the hills roundabout, the motor roared and the bus moved slowly up the street. Raman and Vasanti and Dasan ran alongside, waving to their father, who waved back through the glassless window. With more warning honks of the horn to frighten the chickens and dogs that wandered along the bazaar street, the bus picked up speed, reached the top of the bazaar, swung around the curve in the road, and was gone.

CHAPTER  *FOUR*

When the bus had disappeared, Vasanti and Dasan went off to join their mother at the roadside. Raman turned down the bazaar street and then off onto the little side road that led past the schoolhouse. It was early yet, but perhaps Munuswamy the schoolmaster would be there.

The door of the schoolhouse was open. Raman approached a little uncertainly. The room inside was dim, for it had only one window, and that a small one. Once inside, with eyes accustomed to the dimness, one could see quite well, but for a moment Raman was blinded by the sudden change from the brilliant sunshine outside. He stood still, waiting, until he could see clearly.

The schoolmaster stood with his back toward Raman. As always he was dressed in white — a white *veshti,* or long cotton cloth, wrapped around his waist and falling to his sandals; a long white shirt that came down over the outside of the *veshti;* and a fine white *angavastram,* a kind of fringed scarf that he wore over one shoulder, like an emblem of his respectable position as scholar and teacher.

"Someday," Raman thought, "I too shall wear an *angavastram* like that." He stepped into the room, noiseless on bare feet. The schoolmaster was occupied with adding to the map of India that he had long ago outlined on the whitewashed wall at the front of the room. Raman spoke softly: "Sir." The schoolmaster did not hear. "Sir," repeated Raman, a little louder.

Munuswamy the schoolmaster turned then, somewhat startled. "Eh?" He ducked his head, the better to see through the upper part of his glasses. "Raman? What are you doing here so early?"

"I have come to say that —" Raman swallowed a sudden tightness in his throat "— that I will not be in school any more."

"Not in school?"

"My father has left for the plains," Raman explained, taking care to keep his voice level. "I am needed to help at home."

Munuswamy shook his head. "That is a shame, Raman, a very great shame. But I know that it cannot be helped. Next season you will return, I hope."

Raman nodded. Then his face brightened. "My father has said that for every rupee I earn I may keep one naiya-paisa for myself. That way I will still be able to buy a book to read now and then."

"And how much does a book cost?"

"Tumbuswamy the bookseller sells them for twenty-five naiye-paise."

"So then, how many rupees will you have to earn before you can buy a book?"

"Twenty-five, of course," Raman answered quickly, and thought of the arithmetic lesson he would not be reciting today after all. At the same time he felt a little sinking sensation. Twenty-five rupees! How long would it take to earn such an amount?

Munuswamy the schoolmaster nodded, then smiled. "Look, I am teaching you arithmetic even when you have come to say good-by. Run along now. I must finish my work before it is time for school, and I suppose you must be starting your work also."

Raman nodded. "Good-by, sir."

"Good-by. And while you are reading those books of yours, you might save some time to practice arithmetic as well!"

Raman grinned, touched one hand to his forehead in farewell, and left. When he reached the bazaar street he hesitated, then turned down into the bazaar instead of up toward the top of the hill. Just below the place where the school road joined the main bazaar street, in between the stall of the brass vendor and that of Meerjan the tailor, was a narrow stall lined with shelves and presided over by a thin, stoop-shouldered old man who was, Raman thought, the most fortunate of all the merchants in the bazaar: Tumbuswamy the bookseller.

Actually, Tumbuswamy's little stall contained few books. Its shelves were laden mostly with tattered magazines, all in English, given to him by the Merkin ladies when they left for the plains. Raman wondered who, if anyone, ever bought the magazines. There seemed always to be the same number on the shelves, and certainly few of the hill people could read English.

On one shelf toward the front Tumbuswamy kept the little pile of books like the one Raman had bought — thin, paper-bound booklets printed in Tamil, most of them with finger smudges that betrayed former owners. For twenty-five naiye-paise one could buy a book of animal fables translated from the Sanskrit language of ancient India, or a book of Tamil poems, or a collection of tales about warriors and battles of long ago.

Across the front of Tumbuswamy's stall there was a low counter, and in a glass case at one end of it were the other things that Tumbuswamy sold: pencils and pads of paper and erasers, pen points and ink and a few rulers and copybooks as well, along with slates and pieces of dusty chalk.

Tumbuswamy was busy polishing the glass front of the case when Raman reached his stall.

"Good morning, Tata." Like all the other children who came to the bazaar, Raman addressed the white-haired bookseller as "Grandfather."

"Good morning." Tumbuswamy peered at him, squinting up his eyes because when he looked at Raman he was also looking into the brilliant sunshine that flooded the bazaar outside. "Ah, it's Raman, isn't it? How is it you have come at this hour? Should you not be getting along to school?"

"Starting today, I am working instead of going to school. My father has gone down to the plains."

Raman stood up a little taller as he spoke, conscious of the important sound of the words. "And you know," he went on, excitement creeping into his voice, "Appa has said that I may keep a naiya-paisa for myself out of every rupee I earn while he is gone. That way I can earn enough to buy books."

"A naiya-paisa for every rupee! But you will have to earn many rupees for one book."

"And I'm going to earn many, many of them, you'll see!" Raman swaggered a little. "I only came to tell you, Tata, that I shall be wanting to buy another book one of these days, and to ask if you might have some new ones by then."

"And what kind of book do you think you will want?" Tumbuswamy asked.

"Some more stories of Indian heroes," Raman answered promptly. "Do you think you can get a book like that?"

"It's possible," Tumbuswamy nodded. "Possible."

"I'll be going now," Raman said. "But I'll be back."

"I'm sure you will," Tumbuswamy agreed. "Good luck to you."

Raman raced off up the bazaar street, conscious of the time that had passed since the departure of the bus. Puffing and panting, he reached the top of the street, where the vegetable sellers sat with their wares. His mother was still there, bargaining with a woman who had come to buy vegetables. To a passer-by their voices would sound angry indeed, but Raman knew they were not. It was the custom to bargain. The seller of vegetables must ask more than was expected, and the customer must offer less than he intended to pay. Then, after much arguing, they would agree on the correct price, which was somewhere in between. It was always so. It was a poor merchant or customer who did not bargain.

Raman waited until an agreement had been reached and the customer had departed before he approached. The baby lay sound asleep on a cloth spread on the ground near his mother. Vasanti and Dasan were playing together a little way off. They had found some more *roly-puchis* and were rolling them back and forth like marbles.

"Ah, Raman, it is good you have come." His mother slipped the coins she had just received into a fold of her sari at her waist. "Take Vasanti with you and go back to the house. If the two of you go looking for mushrooms, you may be able to sell them this afternoon. I have heard that a few of the bungalows on the other side of the lake are still occupied. If you don't sell the mushrooms, bring them home and we will dry them."

"Shall I take Dasan also, Amma?"

"No, he can stay here with me. You will be able to gather more if the two of you are alone. Here, take these." She held out three small bananas. "Give one to Vasanti and one to Dasan, and tell Dasan to play where he is and to be sure not to go close to the edge of the road. I should be home by midafternoon, and then we will have rice and pepper water for dinner."

Raman took the bananas and walked over to where the two younger children were playing. A moment later he and Vasanti were on their way home. As they walked up the hill road, Raman cast a sidelong glance toward the place where the path on the edge of the mountain led off to the left. How he would like to follow the path today, to sit on the rock ledge in the sun and look out over the plains, picturing to himself those magnificent armies of long ago! But it would be a long time before he would sit on the ledge again. As though hurrying away from the thought, Raman strode ahead until Vasanti, panting to keep up with him, called to him to wait.

"Enna, where shall we go for the mushrooms?" Vasanti asked when she had come alongside once more.

"The pine shola, perhaps," Raman answered absently. "Or the hill above the park, on the other side of the lake."

"Let's go to the pine shola, then. Last time I found a great many there." When Raman said nothing, Vasanti looked at him shyly. "It is too bad you have to leave school, Raman. I am sorry."

Raman looked straight ahead. "It is nothing," he answered stiffly. "I'll be going back next season."

"You are lucky, Raman, to know how to read. I wish I could." Vasanti's voice was wistful.

Surprised, Raman looked down at his younger sister. Vasanti wanting to read! "Girls have no need for schooling," he said, a trifle scornfully.

"I know. They need only to learn to cook and to keep house." Vasanti repeated words she had heard many, many times, and ended with a sigh.

It was too bad perhaps, thought Raman, feeling pity stir within him. But then, what could be done about it?

He shrugged the thought away from him. The road turned downward now, for they had passed the crest of the hill. With a sudden burst of speed

Raman dashed ahead, calling back to Vasanti, "Thangachi, I'll race you to the house!"

Her momentary wistfulness gone, Vasanti laughed and darted after him, the little glass bangles that she wore around her wrists jingling as she ran.

CHAPTER *FIVE*

After the evening meal Raman sat quietly on the doorstep, where his father had sat the night before, leaning back against the rough wooden frame and watching the sky. It was clear, with a chill wind blowing. The first stars glittered faintly. He could see them out of the corner of his eyes, but when he shifted his gaze to look at them directly they melted away into the soft blue-grayness of the sky.

Vasanti sat nearby, stringing on a thread the mushrooms that had not been sold that afternoon. They would be hung up to dry in the sun the next day. Dried, they could be kept until a market was found for them.

The children's mother came out of the house, where she had been settling the baby for the night. "Vasanti, it is time for you also to be in bed. Dasan is asleep already."

"I'm going now, Amma." Vasanti stood up, brushing off her skirt. "The mushrooms are ready for drying." She handed the strings to her mother and went inside the house.

After the mushrooms were hung from nails driven into the protruding rafters along the side of the house, Raman's mother began the cleaning of the brass rice pot, squatting on the ground not far from Raman, rubbing the sooty sides of the pot with a mixture of sand and ash. Raman watched, wanting to talk with her, especially about his father's farewell promise: the one naiya-paisa Raman was to keep out of each rupee he earned. His mother had not mentioned it, yet she must know of it, for his father had said he had talked with her and that she had agreed — reluctantly perhaps, Raman thought, remembering his father's words: "She perhaps does not understand quite so well . . ." Raman wanted to tell her of the pride, the excitement he felt, but something held the words back. His mother's face, quiet, calm as always, seemed somehow too remote.

His mother was tall for a hill woman. Her black hair was pulled back tightly from her face — so tightly that it seemed to draw the dark skin smooth across her forehead and cheeks — and the thick coil it made at the nape of her neck was smooth and shiny with coconut oil. Her sari, worn and faded as it was, was tied carefully so that the pleats in front and the long end flung back over one shoulder hung just so, and she moved always with easy grace, as when she walked to the town with the vegetable basket balanced on her head.

How many times, thought Raman, had he as a small boy sat thus, watching his mother as she went about her work. She had looked then just as she did now, except — he frowned, reaching back into memory. What was different? Ah, that was it! The nose jewel was missing — the tiny cluster of diamonds that his mother had always worn set above one nostril. As she moved about, the nose jewel had glittered and sparkled, blue-white tinged with rainbow flashes, brilliant against her dark skin. Watching her then, Raman had thought her beautiful. She still was, he decided, especially when she smiled, though that was not often now.

It occurred to Raman that it had been a long time since he had seen the nose jewel. Since before the baby was born? No, long before that surely. The tiny pierced hole where the jewel had set was scarcely visible now. How strange that he had never really noticed the absence of the jewel until now! Had it been lost? No, he would have known of it. And his mother would not keep it hidden, for everyone knew that the safest way to guard jewels was to wear them constantly. The nose jewel must have been sold, then, one winter when money and rice were scarce.

"Money" and "rice": the two words jarred Raman's thoughts back to the present. Today, with their whole basket of mushrooms, he and Vasantí had been able to earn only twenty naiye-paise, and their mother had brought back almost half of her vegetables unsold. For tomorrow, Raman knew, there would be only plain boiled rice for the morning meal. There was not enough money to buy dal to make *dosais*.

The vegetables that grew in their small farming plots were the kinds the Merkin people used. Once in a while, when there was no money in the house and very little rice, they would eat some of the carrots and peas and ears of corn that were not sold. But those vegetables were not the kind for South Indian cooking. And more than anything else they needed rice — piles of white, steaming rice, to fill the stomach and banish hunger — and with the rice just enough spiced curry or pepper water to give a flavor.

Thinking about food, Raman found himself growing hungry again. Just then footsteps sounded on the pathway behind the house. Raman recognized them from their uneven gait. It was his uncle, his father's elder brother, who was slightly lame.

A moment later his uncle appeared around the corner of the house. There were the usual greetings.

"Ah, I am not too well, not too well." Raman's uncle shook his head in answer to Raman's mother's question. "Especially my eyesight. I don't know what is the matter or what I am going to do. Today I received a letter from my son in the city, and I cannot even read it."

He paused expectantly, and Raman's mother said quickly, "Raman can read it for you. Only we have no light here."

"I have a light in my house," Raman's uncle assured her. "If he is free to come."

"Of course." Raman's mother consented immediately.

Raman rose and followed his uncle along the path that led beside the ravine to the house on the slope above his own, where his uncle lived. The scene just passed had been repeated time after time, as though it were a scene from a drama, and all the players knew their parts and knew it was only make-believe. Raman's uncle's eyes were as sharp as any man's, but they had never learned to read. Raman knew it and his mother knew it, and Raman's uncle knew that they knew it, but no one spoke of it.

They reached the one-room cottage, just like Raman's own, in which his uncle lived. His uncle groped in the darkness for a little oil-burning lamp and lighted it. They sat down cross-legged on the floor, and Raman held the letter tilted close to the lamp so that as much light as possible struck the page.

Raman's uncle's son could not write. He must have found a friend who could write the letter for him, or given a few coins to the letter writer in the bazaar to do it. The handwriting was cramped and uneven, and Raman had difficulty in understanding it. When at last he had finished, his eyes ached with the effort to see in the dim, flickering light.

His uncle nodded and folded the letter up again. "Thank you, Raman. Tomorrow I shall answer the letter."

"I'll come in the evening," Raman said, for he knew without asking that his uncle wanted him to write the answer for him. He stood up to take leave.

His uncle also rose and walked to the door with him. The two of them paused a moment in the doorway. Far up the slope beyond his uncle's house a small fire flickered. Figures moved around it, and laughter floated down to where they stood.

"Look, you have just time to join Tata Natesan's circle," Raman's uncle pointed out.

Raman shifted feet uneasily. "Tonight I am not going," he answered, and added hastily, "I am tired today. We went with Appa to the bus in the morning, and since then I have been working."

"Ah, so?" His uncle's eyebrows lifted in surprise. "Well, then, hurry home, before Yellow Eye catches sight of you! Or aren't you afraid of Yellow Eye any more?" There was teasing in his voice.

"Munuswamy the schoolmaster says that Yellow Eye does not exist," Raman answered, and then could have bitten back the words.

"Ah, if your schoolmaster says he does not exist, then all the stories that have been told for so many years must be false, is that it?"

"How can they be true?" Raman pointed out. "No tiger could live for so many years, and with just one eye, too. And besides, only a week ago I saw some Merkin men with packs on their backs who had just returned from climbing the Bearded One, all the way to the top." The Bearded One was the great gaunt mountain that loomed to the north of the hill settlements, sheer and barren except for the wisps of gray and white mist that clung to it and gave it its name. On the slopes of the Bearded One, so the story went, Yellow Eye the tiger roamed, waiting to take revenge upon the hunter who had blinded his eye, or failing that, upon anyone who dared to enter his kingdom.

"So in your school they teach you to scoff as well as to read," his uncle observed, some of the teasing gone from his voice.

"It is not scoffing," Raman said quickly. "It is only finding what is true and what is not."

"Yet not five days ago there was word of a tiger that carried off a young goat from a farm on the edge of a village on the far slope."

"A tiger, yes, but not Yellow Eye. There may be

a few tigers left in the hills, and if they are very hungry they may even come to steal food from an outlying farm. Tata Natesan says that when he was young there were many tigers around here, and other wild beasts as well."

"Tata Natesan also says that Yellow Eye still roams the slopes of the Bearded One, seeking vengeance. One thing you believe, then, and the other you do not?"

"They are not the same thing," Raman insisted stubbornly. "Everyone knows there were many animals in these hills long ago. But who can really believe that a tiger, like a man, will go on seeking revenge for an injury done no one knows how many years ago? And besides, if all that happened when Tata Natesan was a young boy, then Yellow Eye would be almost a hundred years old by now. What tiger could possibly live so long?"

"Your Munuswamy the schoolmaster has taught you well, I see," Raman's uncle observed dryly. "Well, run along now. Yellow Eye or no Yellow Eye, you should hurry home. I have kept you long already."

Raman bade him good night and set off down the path. Yellow Eye indeed! Was it possible that his uncle actually believed the legend of the vengeful tiger? He did not say that he believed, and yet he did not seem pleased that Raman should deny the truth of the story.

Tata Natesan was an old man — some said over a hundred years old — so that even the grownups called him Tata, or "Grandfather." In the daytime he sat quietly in his small hut, or just outside if the weather was good. He was too old to walk the steep hill trails, and there was little or no work that he could do. But at nightfall someone built a little fire for him just outside his hut, and children and grownups alike came to hear him tell his stories. They were stories of animals, mostly, or of happenings in the hills long ago when Tata Natesan was young. Some people said that Tata Natesan's eyes had looked back into the past for so long that they could no longer clearly see the present. But his tongue could weave stories the like of which were not heard elsewhere, and even those who had heard them over and over again came back to listen once more.

Raman glanced back over his shoulder toward the flickering light up on the slope. The laughter and the movement around the fire had died down. Raman could picture the familiar scene: the children would be squatting quietly close around the little circle of warmth, the grownups sitting or standing in the background. Tata Natesan himself would be seated cross-legged on the ground in front of his doorway, wrapped in his old brown blanket, with the firelight deepening the lines that were carved in patterns on his sunken cheeks. His voice was high and thin, but it could cast a spell. No sound would be heard but that voice and the light crackle of the fire.

Until last year Raman had been one of that nightly gathering. The stories had held him spellbound too, above all the tale of Yellow Eye and his vengeful search for the hunter who had wounded him so long ago. Indeed, so vivid did the tale become under the magic of Tata Natesan's words that afterward Raman and the others would scurry home, laughing and jostling one another outwardly, but casting secret glances over their shoulders and out of the corners of their eyes at the shadows along the path, half expecting to see there the outline of that lithe, striped form.

Now Raman knew the tale for what it was — a story and nothing more, useful perhaps for frightening small children into staying close to home after dusk. And with the knowledge some of the magic faded from those stories told around the fire, until at last Raman found himself making excuses for not going there at all. He would be too tired, or too busy with household tasks, or if they were lucky enough to have oil for the lamp, then he would prefer to stay at home and study his lessons. Only to himself did he admit that for him the stories of Tata Natesan had become merely an old man's tales, pale and dull compared with those he read in his books.

Raman wished he had held his tongue when his uncle had brought up the subject of Yellow Eye. He would rather not have admitted his disbelief in the tale of the dreaded tiger — at least not to his uncle, of all people. His uncle might easily misinterpret Raman's words and find in them proof that his own predictions were beginning to come true. For it was his uncle who had objected in the beginning, the year before, when Raman's father had made known his plans to send his son to school.

Raman remembered well that evening a year ago. He had already gone to bed when his Uncle Raju had arrived to join Raman's father outside the doorstep of their house. The men's voices, low at first, had risen gradually until, quite without wanting to, Raman had been able to hear them.

"You do not foresee the outcome," Raman's

uncle had said. "His head will be filled with learning, and it will make him dissatisfied with all of this: with his home, his village, his family, his whole life."

"Perhaps," Raman's father had answered slowly, "perhaps I would want him to be dissatisfied. Why should I insist that he become a woodcutter merely because I am one?"

"It is not that I am opposed to schooling," Raman's uncle went on, hardly seeming to hear Raman's father's answer. "Have I not wished many times that I too had learned to read and write? But remember that Raman will be the first in our village, the only one, who has gone to school. It will set him apart from the rest, and he will no longer be one of us. He will become scornful of those who have not had the chance to learn. Better instead to wait, for one day we will surely have our own school here in the village, and then Raman and the others will all learn together, and there will be no difficulty."

"I have waited," Raman's father pointed out. "Is Raman not twelve years old already? I would have sent him to school many years ago had it been possible. People have talked of having a school in our settlement since you and I were children, and what has come of it? Where is the money for the schoolhouse or for the salary of the schoolmaster? Our people do well to have enough to buy food. We did not learn to read, you and I. We did not have the chance. But I am fortunate; this year has been a good year, and we can do without Raman's help during the day. I want him to have this chance while he can."

And so it had gone on, while Raman crouched tensely under his blanket in the dark room, wishing he could not hear, yet anxious to know his father's reply. For Raju was the elder brother, and it was customary for the younger brother to take the advice of the elder. Nevertheless, Raman's father held fast to his purpose, and at last Raju had risen with a sigh.

"Very well then. I can see your mind is made up. But I am afraid for the boy's happiness. It is a fine thing to learn, but I wish he were not the first. It is never an easy thing to be the first."

With those words he had left, and Raman had breathed deeply, feeling the tenseness slip away and the warmth of relief flood over him. How close he had been to losing his dream of going to school! His uncle was mistaken, of course. How could learning to read and write cut him off from his family, his village, all that was familiar to him? He would prove his uncle's predictions to be wrong. Never would his uncle have a chance to say, "I told you so!"

Yet Raman had come close to giving his uncle that chance tonight. If his uncle knew that Raman no longer went to Tata Natesan's fireside, he would be sure to interpret this as evidence that Raman was "drifting away" from the others. He would not understand that it was merely that the stories seemed less interesting now that Raman had his books instead. Perhaps it was fortunate after all that the subject of Yellow Eye had come up. It had distracted his uncle's attention from the excuse Raman had made for not going to the fireside. Only Raman wished that he had not spoken out quite so strongly against the tale of the one-eyed tiger.

Raman had reached his own house. There was no sign of anyone about. All must have gone to bed, so that they might be up at dawn the next day. He groped his way inside.

One corner of the room was Raman's own. Here he kept the palm mat that was his bed — rolled up and leaned against the wall by day, spread out on the earthen floor at night. Here also he kept his most cherished possessions — the little pile of books, all similar in size and appearance to the one he had been reading the day before, all worn from many, many thumbings. And finally, here in the wall, close to the floor, was the loose mud brick behind which Raman had dug a little hollow to serve as a hiding place for the coins he saved in order to buy books. No one knew of the hiding place but Raman himself, for he did not open it except when it was dark and no one could see. Now, when he had reached the corner, Raman knelt down and pried the loose brick out of its place. The coin his father had given him at the bus stand was tied in a corner of his shirttail for safekeeping. Fumbling in the darkness, Raman worked the knot loose and took out the coin. He felt inside the hollow in the wall for the bit of cloth that lay there, and drew it out. Carefully he wrapped the coin in the cloth and then stuffed it back into the hiding place. He replaced the brick and felt with his hands to be sure that it was evenly set and did not stick out beyond the others.

With a sigh, Raman straightened up and reached for his rolled-up mat. He laid it on the floor and gave it a kick so that it unrolled itself and lay flat. Then he unfolded his blanket and wrapped it around him. He lay down, curving one arm under his head for a pillow, and fell asleep.

CHAPTER  *SIX*

Three weeks passed slowly by — three weeks in which no word came from Raman's father, which must mean that he had not yet found work. Each day it seemed the ration of rice grew less, though there were plenty of garden vegetables, because almost none could be sold. Raman and Vasanti gathered mushrooms until there was no more room to hang the strings on which they dried. They tried picking berries to sell, but there was no market for them. They filled big burlap bags with pine cones and sold them for kindling. And still it was not enough.

There must be some other way, Raman thought. He was sitting on the rock ledge above the path on the edge of the mountain for the first time since the day his father had left. He looked out over the plains, but this time he did not see armies of elephants and chariots. He saw only the shimmering pattern of fields and ponds far below, and off in the distance the misty blur that was the city where his father was. His gaze left the plains and rested on the slopes below the path, where lantana shrubs grew thickly, bright with pink and yellow flowers and the shiny little black berries that the birds loved to eat. From where he sat he could see a pair of bulbuls hopping from bush to bush, gorging themselves on the round black fruit. They were soft, gray-and-white birds with tall crests and splashes of scarlet across each cheek, and they chattered and chortled musically as they feasted.

In among the lantana grew other flowers, wanderers from the gardens of the Merkin bungalows up on the cliff above. Forming the words silently, Raman named them: larkspur, foxgloves, snapdragons, purple sage. Strange-tasting English words! He had learned them from his Uncle Raju, who had worked as a gardener in one of the Merkin bungalows before he had become lame. When he was younger, Raman had sometimes helped his uncle tend the flower beds, setting out the young plants, tying up drooping stems, cutting flowers for the big brass vases in the bungalow.

Raman sat up straight suddenly. An idea had come, vaguely at first. The flowers — was there something he could do with the flowers? Sell them perhaps? Most of the bungalows had their own gardens, but still . . . there might be a bungalow where the flowers were not in bloom; or there might be someone who would buy the flowers anyway, if they were nicely picked and arranged.

It was worth a try. Raman descended hastily to the path, and from there made his way cautiously down the slope beyond. Eagerly he began to pick the flowers, breaking off long straight stems as he had seen his uncle do. When he had as many stalks as he could carry, he scrambled back up the slope to the path again. Tilting back his head, he peered upward toward the white bungalows that stood on the hill above, overlooking the plains. He would try there first.

He walked along the path until he came to an iron gate, beyond which rose a flight of stone steps leading up toward the bungalow above. Raman lifted the latch and opened the gate just enough to slip through, then carefully closed it again. How cold the steps were to his feet! The wind stung his bare legs as he climbed. Sometimes his feet slipped where the stones were damp and green with moss.

But when he reached the top and stood before the bungalow, he saw that it was deserted, the windows shuttered and the doors padlocked. It was the same with the next bungalow, and the next. On he trudged, until the flowers began to wilt from the warmth of his clenched hand. It was no use. If only he had had this idea before!

But there! At the top of the hill, just before the road curved away toward the farm settlements, there was one house from whose chimney a wisp of smoke curled upward. Someone was still there. Raman broke into a run. "Please let them want the flowers. Please let them want the flowers." It was a little prayer whispered under his breath as he ran.

The chimney from which the smoke rose upward belonged, not to the main bungalow, but to the small cookhouse just behind it. Peeking through the door of the cookhouse, Raman saw a white-turbaned cook stirring something in a pan on the big iron stove. Raman knew the cook by name, for he had seen him in the bazaar many times. He was called Big Sundaram, and he came from the plains every year with the Merkin lady for whom he worked. He was tall and very broad, but stoop-shouldered from bending over the stove for so many, many years, peering into the pots and pans that boiled there.

Big Sundaram looked up as Raman's shadow darkened the doorway.

"What is it, boy?" His speech was Tamil, but not the Tamil of the hills.

"I have come to see if Madam will buy flowers." Raman held out the bouquet in his hand.

"Madam is on the veranda," answered Sundaram, picking up a flat wooden stick and stirring something in another one of the pots on the stove. "But I do not think she will want to buy flowers." He gestured toward the outdoors with his stick. "Look around you, boy. Have you seen gardens to equal these?"

Raman looked toward the house. He saw larkspur taller than he was, pink and blue lilies crowded together along the drive, snapdragons and slender-stemmed poppies in brilliant patches of color all around the yard, and many other flowers whose names he did not even know. The flowers he was holding seemed to droop in comparison, and the hand that grasped them fell down to his side until they trailed in the dust. He turned to go.

"But wait," Big Sundaram said, more kindly. "You may ask Madam if you wish. Come with me." He poked two more sticks into the mouth of the big stove, wiped his hands on the towel he wore slung over his shoulder, and then came out, frowning in the sunlight that was so bright compared to the dim, windowless kitchen. Raman followed him across the courtyard and around to the other side of the bungalow.

The Merkin lady was sitting on the veranda, facing the other direction, so that only her gray hair showed above the back of her big chair. Raman stared at the chair. It had big wheels instead of legs.

"Madam, this boy brings flowers to sell." Big Sundaram spoke in Tamil. At the sound of his voice the Merkin lady swung the chair around on its wheels, and Raman saw that she had one leg encased in white plaster. He remembered that his uncle had had just such a cast on his leg when first it had been injured. Quickly he lowered his gaze, abashed, lest the Merkin lady think him rude for staring. He did not see the Merkin lady smile as she shook her head.

"I don't need flowers. I have plenty in my own

garden." She spoke in Tamil also, but the slowness with which she said the words gave them a strange sound in Raman's ears.

Raman nodded, eyes still downcast. It was as Big Sundaram had said. Why should the Merkin lady want his poor flowers, that were nothing compared with those in her own compound?

But as he turned to go, struggling to keep the disappointment from showing in his face, the Merkin lady spoke again. "Wait, boy, I have another idea." Raman turned, wondering. "There are flowers that I would like to have. But they are not garden flowers. They are flowers of the hills." She paused, and in the silence Raman dared to look straight at her, and found himself gazing into very bright, very blue eyes that searched his face keenly, but with kindness. "Do you know the flowers I mean?"

Raman tried to think. Hill flowers? There were, surely, small flowers growing wild here and there, in the sholas, or groves, beyond the lake. But they would not do to keep in a vase. Certainly they could not be the ones the Merkin lady wanted.

"I am not sure," Raman answered at last. "I have not noticed them."

"Look for them, then," said the Merkin lady. "And if you find them, bring them to me."

Raman nodded. "I will try, Amma." The Tamil word for "mother" was used as a respectful form of address to any older woman.

He took leave then, with a farewell salute, and hurried off, tossing the wilted bouquet of flowers away as soon as he was outside the gate. It was dusk already, and too late to look for any hill flowers today. Tomorrow he would try the pine shola. It was a shaded place, and surely a good one for flowers to grow in. He had never noticed any

70

flowers there, but then he had not been looking for them. Tomorrow he would search in earnest. Let Vasanti spend her time gathering pine cones and mushrooms! Raman would find the hill flowers for the Merkin lady and earn perhaps much more. Who could tell?

He turned off onto the narrow path that was a short cut from the road to the ravine where his house stood. So absorbed was he in his thoughts that he did not see the figure coming up the path toward him. The figure stopped, but Raman did not, and in a moment he had collided with the boy who stood, hands in his pockets, feet apart, in the middle of the path.

Raman choked back a startled exclamation. It was Jesu-Dasan, who had been Raman's closest friend until last year. The two boys stood looking at each other, faces set in hard lines.

"You have indeed become a scholar now," Jesu-Dasan said then, mockery in his voice. "Is it not a sign of the true scholar to be so absent-minded that you do not see where you are going?"

"I was thinking of something else," Raman said stiffly, moving to one side to step past the other boy.

But Jesu-Dasan took a step also to block

Raman's way. Though of Raman's age, he was taller, stockier of build.

"We meet so seldom these days," Jesu-Dasan went on. "We do not even see you at Tata Natesan's fireside any more."

Raman said nothing.

"Now that you can read, it is beneath you to go there, right?"

"That is not so." Rising anger choked Raman's voice. "I am too busy."

"Too busy!" Jesu-Dasan mimicked. "Too busy! Before you went to school you were not too busy. You mean you are too good for us now! You can read, and we cannot. You are the scholar, and we are only farm boys. Isn't it so?" Jesu-Dasan's voice was harsh now.

"I am busy, that's all," Raman repeated stubbornly.

Another figure was coming up the path behind Jesu-Dasan. "Let's go, Enna, it's getting late!" called a new voice.

"Look who's here!" Jesu-Dasan called back over his shoulder. "It's the Scholarly One. Should we not salute him as we pass by?"

"Oh, come on," the other boy retorted impatiently. "We won't be back in time for Tata Natesan's

72

fire at this rate."

Jesu-Dasan shrugged then and stepped aside with exaggerated politeness, bowing and touching a hand to the middle of his forehead in a mocking salute. Head held stiffly erect, Raman stepped past, walking down the trail with measured steps, resisting the temptation to break into a run.

"Hail to the Scholar!" Jesu-Dasan's mocking voice followed him. "Salute the Scholarly One!" Then the taunts faded as the other two boys hurried on up the path.

That night Raman lay awake for a long time on his palm mat, hearing against his will the taunting words of Jesu-Dasan echoing in his mind. If only he had been looking down the path, he would have seen Jesu-Dasan coming, and he could have turned aside and cut across the slope and so avoided the meeting. Jesu-Dasan would no doubt have jeered at him anyway, but at least they wouldn't have met face to face.

Raman thought back to the time when Jesu-Dasan had been his closest friend, and the two of them, along with the other boys from the settlement, had spent untold hours, after the day's work was done, playing in the nearby ravines and clearings or rolling hoops along the hill roads. When

Raman had first started to school, he had still found time to join the others after his chores were done and his lessons prepared, and after their play all would go together to Tata Natesan's fire. But then Raman had begun to spend more and more time on his lessons, anxious as he was to catch up with the other pupils his own age. He would go off by himself as soon as his household tasks were finished, to practice reading from one of his schoolbooks or to find a quiet spot with a smooth patch of ground where he could write with a stick the letters and words he had learned in school. Only when the daylight had faded, and he could no longer see to read or write, would he put aside his lessons and go join the others to hear the stories around the fire.

Then, little by little, Raman had found that Tata Natesan's stories had lost their magic for him. It was more fun, really, to sit at home, even when there was no light, to think over the stories that he had read, retelling them to himself, adding to them from his own imagination, picturing the life he would lead when one day he had become the scholar he longed to be. So when Jesu-Dasan and the others called him to join them, he would make one excuse or another and keep to himself instead.

"Why can't you come this time?" Jesu-Dasan had demanded late one afternoon, when Raman had refused to join in a hoop race on the road before time for Tata Natesan's fire.

"I have to study," Raman had explained. "We began a new book today —"

Jesu-Dasan cut him short. "Why don't you just come right out and say it? Why not say that you just don't want to come because now you can read and that makes you better than we are?"

"That's not true," Raman protested. "I'd like to come — some other time."

"Some other time! Always some other time! You have said that already more times than I can count. Do you think we don't understand why you've changed? Well, if you'd rather have your books, you can keep them, and welcome!" And Jesu-Dasan strode away up the path without a backward glance.

Raman had watched him go, sorry for the refusal that he might, after all, have avoided. Next time I'll go with them, he decided. But there had been no next time.

For several days Raman had not seen Jesu-Dasan at all. And then one day he had made up his mind to go and seek the other boy out, perhaps even to say that he was sorry if his refusal had hurt Jesu-Dasan's feelings. He had set off up the slope toward Jesu-Dasan's house. Halfway there he had caught sight of Jesu-Dasan and the others, and he was about to hurry over to join them when suddenly Jesu-Dasan had cupped his hands around his mouth and shouted out, "Look, there goes the bookworm now! Hail to the Scholar, the Scholarly One!" Then he had made his mocking bow and salute, and because he was the leader, the other boys had joined in.

Sick with the shock of the unexpected taunts, Raman had gone on, pretending that his destination lay elsewhere. After that he did all he could to avoid meeting Jesu-Dasan, all the while pretending indifference to the mocking cries that would pursue him from the distance. Until today he had not come again face to face with the other boy.

What had made Jesu-Dasan and the other boys turn against him? "Jealousy," Raman thought. "They are jealous because I have the chance to go to school and they do not."

But in his heart he knew there was another answer.

"It will set him apart from the rest, and he will

no longer be one of us." Those had been his uncle's words. But it was not learning to read and write that had created the trouble.

"It was my own fault, really," Raman thought heavily. "Not the fault of the schooling, and not the fault of the other boys either. There were times, many times, when I could have played with them, only it seemed more fun to read or practice for school. I could have gone to Tata Natesan's fire, too, even though I wouldn't have enjoyed the stories so much any more. Jesu-Dasan knew I was just making excuses, and who can blame him for feeling hurt? Only . . . couldn't he understand how I felt about the schooling? It was so exciting, especially at first, and I wanted to do well and to catch up with the others in my class, and then I would have spent less time with my books and more time with the other boys."

He wondered how much his father or his uncle knew of the trouble between him and Jesu-Dasan. They could not be entirely ignorant of it, surely. At least not his uncle, who because of his lame foot spent most of his time at home. No — probably the whole settlement had heard Jesu-Dasan's shouted mockery. Even now Raman's uncle might be telling himself that this, too, proved the truth of his prediction.

"But I know it doesn't," Raman told himself. "I know it was right for my father to send me to school. I didn't want to lose Jesu-Dasan's friendship. I didn't realize what was happening until it was too late. But it is really my own fault, and not the fault of the schooling."

He wished there were something he could do to regain the other boy's friendship. But he could never, never approach Jesu-Dasan now. The echo of those mocking cries would keep him from it. Between the two of them, once the closest of friends, there was now a rift that neither of them could bridge.

"In one thing my uncle was right, after all," Raman thought miserably. "It is not an easy thing to be the first."

He shifted his position so that his throbbing forehead rested on the curve of his arm and turned his thoughts with an effort away from Jesu-Dasan to the Merkin lady and the hill flowers he, Raman, would search for, and surely find, the next day. When at last he slept, it was to dream of a forest filled with strange and beautiful flowers the like of which he had never seen. Flowers for the Merkin lady! But each time he bent to pick one it would

78

disappear, until at last, alone in a forest barren of blossoms, he flung himself on the ground and sobbed aloud.

CHAPTER ❦ *SEVEN*

For once Raman was eager to set out on the daily search for pine cones. He had told no one about the hill flowers, wanting instead to find them and surprise the others with the money he would earn. He could not expect, anyway, to be excused from gathering cones in order to undertake a search that had no promise of success. Once he had proved that he could earn money by finding flowers, he would surely be allowed to devote his time to that instead. But for now, at least, the gathering of the pine cones would take him away from the settlements and the bungalows, so that any flowers he might find were sure to be wild, and not strays from some bungalow garden.

Empty bags slung over their shoulders, Raman and Vasanti walked up the ravine away from their settlement, up to the pine shola, where the trees formed a thick grove and the needles matted the ground below and made it springy beneath their feet. The strong monsoon wind had blown many of the cones to the ground. Vasanti set about filling her bag at once. Raman worked more slowly, restless with the thought of the hill flowers he must find. Each time he bent to pick up a cone, his gaze wandered about, searching for some sign of the flowers. He saw none.

Strange, he had never really noticed before how few plants grew here. Those that did were scanty, low-growing, and without blossoms. Perhaps they did not get enough sun here. Raman fought down his discouragement. He had thought it would be so easy to find the hill flowers!

There were many other places he could try, of course. But by the time the cones were gathered and sold, it would be late afternoon, almost evening, and there would be no time left to go off hunting flowers. What could he do?

By the time they stopped to rest, Vasanti had filled her two bags. Raman had finished one and had only started the second. They left the bags leaning against a tree trunk and walked to the bottom of the ravine to drink from the little stream that ran there. Along the stream bed it was more open, and the stream banks were thickly grown with vines and ferns. The children squatted beside the stream, resting and eating some of the purple berries that still clung to the vines.

"Just imagine, Raman," Vasanti said, squinting upward at the trees on the ravine slope above them, "when Tata Natesan was a young boy, these trees were not here at all. There was only grass and wild animals, and a wet swamp where the lake is now."

"I know," Raman nodded. "I have heard him tell about it. The Merkin people who came here planted the pine trees and the blue gum trees, and built the bungalows and blocked up the streams to make the lake." It was a revival of the old game they had played so often. Each of them in turn would name something in the hills that had not been there when Tata Natesan was a boy: the fruit orchards, the pine sholas, the white bungalows, the farm settlements, the vegetable fields, the lake itself. Then they would think of things that had been there when Tata Natesan was a boy and were now gone, or nearly so: the open grassy slopes, the reedy marsh where three streams flowed together, the tigers and perhaps occasional elephants and many other wild animals. This game had whiled away many hours for them as they worked or rested. But today Raman's response was halfhearted, and Vasanti, sensing his reluctance to join in, was silent then, lost in her own thoughts.

Raman shifted from his squatting position to a sitting one, and then rolled over and lay on his stomach, propping his head up with his elbows. He sniffed the fragrance of the damp earth. There was a pink blur in front of him, and when his eyes focused upon it, it sharpened into the outlines of a flower — a tiny one, to be sure, but lovely and delicate, with faint tracings of violet on its petals.

A hill flower.

Raman sat bold upright. "There's one, right there!" he exclaimed out loud. Vasanti stared. Raman reached out and picked the flower, pinching off the slender stem at its base. This was a hill flower, a kind not to be found in any garden. Why the Merkin lady should want it, when her own garden was crowded with beautiful blossoms of every color, was a mystery indeed. But there was no doubt in Raman's mind that this was the kind of flower the Merkin lady had meant. He looked around him, searching the dense foliage keenly. There was another one, over there. And another. On hands and knees he crept along the stream bank, gathering flowers as he went.

He was suddenly conscious of Vasanti's astonished gaze. "Vasanti, take your bags of cones back. I'll come later!" he called.

"But what about yours?" Vasanti protested.

"Never mind. I'll be coming. Go quickly." Vasanti hesitated only a moment more, then turned and scrambled up the ravine slope. Raman watched a trifle guiltily as she lifted the two bags of pine cones onto her thin shoulders. The bags were not so heavy, but they were bulky and hard to carry, and the pine cones were prickly and scratched through the loosely woven burlap. But soon Vasanti was out of sight, and Raman turned his attention back to the flowers. He walked slowly up the stream bed, picking each flower he saw, until he had as many as he could carry in two hands.

He would not be able to take the bags of pine cones. They would be safe here, leaning against the tree trunk, until he could come back for them. The flowers were more important. For so many of them he would surely be paid well. The Merkin lady would praise him for finding so many, for they grew well hidden in the thick foliage, and it required careful searching to spot them.

Leaning forward, balancing himself by waving his arms because he could not use his hands, Raman started straight up the steepest part of the slope. There was no time to lose by going the long way around. Already some of the first flowers he had found were beginning to wilt.

By the time he reached the big bungalow on the hill, the flowers were a sorry sight indeed. The petals were crumpled and closed, and the slender stems drooped lifelessly. Raman's steps slowed as he approached the veranda of the bungalow. He put his hands behind his back, half ashamed to show the flowers.

The Merkin lady was in her wheelchair on the veranda, as she had been on the previous day, facing the end of the veranda from which one could see the plains that stretched below the path on the edge of the mountain. She did not turn, for Raman's bare feet made no sound as he came around the corner of the house.

"Amma." Raman spoke uncertainly, suddenly shy.

The Merkin lady turned. "Yes?"

"I have brought the hill flowers, Amma. But —"
He stopped, and wordlessly held out the flowers.

"Oh, what a shame! They're all dead!"

"I brought them from very far, Amma. And
while I was coming they became like this."

The Merkin lady held out her hand and took the
flowers. "I can't use them this way." She shook her
head. "And look, this is one I especially wanted."
She sighed and was silent a moment. Raman stood
uneasily, cautiously scratching one leg with his
other foot. Somewhere in hunting for the flowers
he had brushed up against a plant that made his
skin itch.

"It is too bad," the Merkin lady was saying, half
to herself. "I really did not expect . . . but if you
are serious about bringing the flowers, then we
must think of something . . . Listen, boy — what is
your name: Raman? — listen, Raman, go out behind the cookhouse and see if there is a small
basket there. Bring it to me, and tell Sundaram to
come also."

Raman hastened to obey. The basket was easily
found. There were many of them, piled there after
being brought from the market. He chose one and
went to call Sundaram from the kitchen.

The Merkin lady spoke to Sundaram briefly, this time in English, making digging gestures with one hand as she talked. Big Sundaram nodded and left, returning in a few minutes with a small digging tool — a "trowel" the Merkin lady called it. Raman had seen his uncle use just such a tool when he worked in the bungalow gardens. It was like a miniature shovel, useful for digging up weeds without disturbing the surrounding plants, or for making small holes for setting out young garden plants.

"Now then," the Merkin lady went on in her slow, careful Tamil, "listen carefully, Raman. When you find a flower, do not pick it. Dig up the plant instead, and put it in the basket, with enough earth to cover the roots. Sprinkle some water if you can, to keep it fresh. Do you understand?"

Raman nodded. "I understand. Amma wants the whole plant, with roots and leaves, and not just the flower alone."

"That's right. And one thing more, Raman. It will be better if you do not bring more than four plants in one day, at the very most. I cannot use so many at one time. And be sure that each plant is a new kind. You will have to remember which kinds you have brought. I do not want the same kind of flower twice."

"I will do that, Amma." Raman picked up the basket and the trowel and took leave with a respectful salute.

It was getting late. Raman was hungry, but he did not want to go home. How could he, when in the whole day he had earned no money at all? When he had reached a place along the road not far from his house, he hid the basket and the trowel carefully in some bushes where they would be safe until he could return for them. Then he made his way back to the pine shola and found the bags of pine cones where he had left them. Quickly he worked to fill the second bag, then hoisted both bags up onto his back and started back toward the road. He must find someone to buy the cones.

It was after sunset when at last Raman reached his own cottage. The pine cones had been sold, finally, but for only fifteen naiye-paise a bag, instead of the usual twenty-five. For his whole day's work he had only thirty naiye-paise — not even half a rupee!

His mother was inside the house, stirring the pot of rice set over the fire.

"I have come back, Amma," Raman announced

when he stood beside her.

"You must be hungry, having eaten nothing since morning." His mother's face was hidden from him. Her voice was quiet and even, yet Raman felt reproach behind it. Quickly he blurted out the story of the hill flowers.

"Here is the money for the cones, Amma," he ended, holding out the coins. His mother took them in her hand, looked at them with speaking, and tucked them into the fold at the waistline of her sari.

"Wash now, my son. The rice is ready. Tell Vasanti and Dasan to wash also."

The dinner was plain rice, thinned with water to make it seem like more. Raman longed for some hot pepper water or some curried vegetables to cover the flat rice taste. Dasan took a few mouthfuls and wrinkled his nose.

"Amma, I don't like the rice plain like this."

"That is all we have today. We have no spices to make curry." Did she glance in Raman's direction? Raman bent his head and scooped up the rice porridge in his cupped palm as quickly as possible. As soon as he could, he left the house and went to wash his hands again, then sat off by himself at the back of the house, leaning up against the mud-brick wall, watching the beginning flicker of lights from those cottages whose inhabitants were lucky enough to have oil for their lamps.

Today things had not gone well. In his eagerness to get the flowers for the Merkin lady, Raman had neglected his real work. He should have sold the pine cones first, before looking for the flowers. His mother said nothing, but he knew she felt it was so. If only he had had something to show for the time spent in gathering the flowers! But the Merkin lady could scarcely be expected to pay for flowers that were dead and useless when she received them; nor could she know that, in looking for the flowers, Raman had lost part of the money he should have earned by selling the cones.

Tomorrow would go better, Raman promised himself. The basket and the trowel were tucked away safely in his corner of the room. Tomorrow there would be no mistakes.

CHAPTER ~ *EIGHT*

It was late afternoon when Raman arrived once more at the bungalow on the hill, carrying his basket hung on a rope slung over his sholder. Today he had made certain that the pine cones were gathered and sold first. Fifty naiye-paise were knotted in a corner of his shirttail. Now more coins would soon join them. There would be no cause for reproach this time!

It had not been so easy to find the flowers today. He had gone again to the stream below the pine shola, but he had picked all the flowers there the day before, and he could not tell which plants were which without the flowers. Besides, he was sure that the Merkin lady would want only the plants that were in bloom. He had wandered farther up the ravine, clear up to the waterfall, before he had found more flowers. He had brought back four plants: one with pale lavender blossoms, one with pink, and two different white ones. He had dug them up carefully and pressed earth around their roots in the basket, and then sprinkled them with water that he scooped from the stream in his cupped palms. Now a peek inside the basket assured him that all was well. The plants were as fresh as when he had first found them. He could be proud of the flowers he brought today.

The Merkin lady was indeed pleased. "You have done well, Raman. You have followed the instructions exactly." She set the basket down on the floor beside her chair and reached into a pocket of her gown. She drew out a small purse and opened it. "Come here, Raman." Raman obeyed. The Merkin lady reached out one hand, and Raman held his two hands out, touching each other, palms cupped slightly — the respectful way to receive anything from another person. The Merkin lady dropped four coins into his hands: twenty-five naiye-paise for each plant — one rupee in all. A whole rupee! Raman could not keep his eyes from rounding with delight.

The Merkin lady smiled. "Bring the flowers whenever you can, Raman. Just be sure each one you bring is a new kind that you have not brought before. For each new one you shall have twenty-five naiye-paise. All right?"

"All right," Raman grinned.

"I think I shall start work right now; there is still light," the Merkin lady went on, murmuring to herself in English. Raman waited, not understanding the words but sensing that he had not yet been dismissed. "Raman," she said in Tamil, "before you go, will you go into the house and bring me a box that you will find on the table on the other side of the room?"

"A box, Amma?"

"A large flat box." She gestured to show the size.

Raman nodded and entered the house. It was the first time he had ever been inside one of the Merkin bungalows. He found himself in a large room with many windows that looked out toward the plains. There was a great deal of furniture in the room: a sofa, several plump armchairs, a table with armless chairs around it. In Raman's house the only "furniture" was the palm mats that the family slept on and that were rolled up each morning out of the way. He tried to imagine how it would feel to sit in one of those thickly padded chairs. It would be strange, surely!

There was a huge stone fireplace at one end of the room, but it was not the fireplace that drew Raman's gaze and held it in that direction. It was the shelves that lined the walls on either side of the fireplace: shelf upon shelf upon shelf, all full of books. There were books of every size and description — not thin, grimy, paper-covered booklets like those Raman read, but thick books with covers that were brightly colored or dark and richly engraved with gold letters and designs. Forgetful of his errand, Raman approached the shelves slowly, staring. To own such books, to read such books! What must it be like?

"That is the kind of books I shall have someday," Raman told himself dazedly. What scholar could be bothered with those cheap, paper-covered booklets that Tumbuswamy the bookseller sold? They were scarcely worthy of the name "book."

"Can you find the box, Raman?" It was the Merkin lady's voice. With a start, Raman remembered his errand. The box was over there, on the table by the window. He hurried over, picked up the box carefully, slipping both arms underneath so that it would remain level, and turned back toward the door that led to the veranda. With one more glance — just one more — at the wonderful array of books, Raman left the room.

"Now," said the Merkin lady, taking the box from Raman and resting it across her knees, "see if you can bring that table over here, Raman." She indicated a table set against the wall at the far end of the veranda. It was too heavy to lift, but Raman pulled it into place in front of the wheelchair. Then he stood back, watching in silence while the Merkin lady opened the box. She took out a few slender brushes and several small metal tubes with colored labels. Looking up, she smiled at Raman's curious gaze. "Only one thing more, Raman. I need a plate and a glass of water from the cookhouse. Sundaram is not there. You'll have to find them yourself."

It was not difficult. In a moment Raman was back. The Merkin lady had taken one of the plants out of the basket and set it on the table, pressing the damp earth around its roots to hold it erect. A small board that had been in the bottom of the box was lying on the table now, with a piece of white paper fastened over it. The Merkin lady took the plate and glass from Raman and put them on the table also. She picked up one of the tubes, opened it, and squeezed it. A thin, dark green paste oozed out. From another tube she squeezed some blue, and from another some brown, and from still another some yellow, until there was a row of colored daubs on the white surface of the plate. Then with a brush dipped in water she began to mix the colors, until the bright, hard green of the paint became the soft, grayed green of the leaves of the plant in front of her. She dipped a brush in the newly mixed green and, with deft strokes, applied it to the paper on the board.

Before Raman's astonished eyes there began to take shape on the paper the very image of the plant he had brought. Wondering, he watched until the picture was completed, down to the finest of purple veins that lined the delicate petals of the flower. At last the Merkin lady sat back in her chair and put the brushes down on the table. She looked at Raman and smiled.

"So now, Raman, you know why I wanted the hill flowers. And why I must have them fresh, not wilted."

Raman nodded. "It's very good, Amma," he ventured to add.

"Thank you, Raman. With your help I hope to make many more like this. But now it is too late to work more today. There is not enough light. I hope the plants will stay fresh until tomorrow morning."

"I'll put more water on them, Amma," Raman offered quickly.

"Thank you, Raman. That's a good idea." It was the work of moments to take the basket to the water tap out in the compound, and sprinkle the plants with water once again. When Raman returned, the Merkin lady was just putting away the brushes and the paint tubes. Raman sprang forward to return the table to its former place as soon as it was cleared. The Merkin lady nodded an acknowledgment. "Now, then, Raman, you had better take another basket from behind the cookhouse to use in place of this one. You may go now, and thank you for your help."

"Good night, Amma. I will go and come." Raman bade farewell with the traditional Tamil phrase. He went in search of the basket to replace the one left with the plants, and then hurried down the drive toward the road. Already it was twilight, and his mother would wonder what had delayed him. He could picture her surprise when he gave her the money. One rupee and fifty naiyepaise he had earned today — the most for any single day so far! Best of all, it meant a naiya-paisa for himself, to add to the small pile of coins he kept tucked away behind the loose brick. There were eleven naiye-paise there now. This would make twelve. And he could make a mark on the wall, too, to show that there was a half-rupee extra earned, so that next time he earned a half-rupee he could add the two together and have still another naiya-paisa for his own.

He broke into a run, feeling how the coins tied in the corner of his shirttail bounced against his body as he jogged along the road. One rupee and fifty naiye-paise! And the promise of many more to come!

For supper there was rice with a little pepper water. Raman broke the customary silence during the meal in order to tell the story of the Merkin lady and the flowers, and the pictures the Merkin lady painted that were so real they looked like the flowers themselves growing on paper.

His mother listened quietly. She had been pleased with the extra money earned, though not as surprised and delighted as Raman had hoped. Now she shook her head, wondering that the Merkin lady would pay money simply for small wild plants that were in bloom, and then only in order to paint pictures of them.

"But of course we are lucky that she is willing to do so," she added quickly, sensing Raman's disappointment. "It will be a great help to us."

Raman nodded, wishing his mother shared more of his excitement. She was even quieter than usual. She must be worried, he decided. It was more than three weeks now, with no word from his father.

It seemed to Raman that time passed so slowly. Would the younger children never go to bed? But Vasanti's blanket had torn again, and she wept with discouragement because the more she tried to mend it, the more it tore. Finally their mother took the blanket and sewed the hole up herself as best she could. Then Vasanti and Dasan went off to bed, and soon after that Raman's mother lay down beside the already sleeping baby. Raman spread out his palm mat in his own corner of the room and listened for the deep, regular breathing that would tell him that the others were asleep. Then he inched himself over to the wall and felt along it until his fingers found the ridge made by the edge of the loose brick. He worked the brick out of its place and reached into the hollow behind it for the bit of cloth in which the coins were wrapped. The cloth was there, but it was curiously light in weight. Empty. But it couldn't be!

Raman sat bolt upright in the dark. The cloth was empty, there was no doubt about it. He grubbed frantically in the little hollow to find whether the coins had somehow fallen out. His fingers felt only dust. He lifted the edge of his palm mat and felt along the rough dirt floor. He went back to the hollow in the wall again, but it was no use. The money was gone.

Numbly Raman slid the brick back into place. What could have happened to the coins? Vasanti? She would never . . . but who else? He had been sure that no one knew his hiding place, but perhaps Vasanti had seen him there sometime when he had thought her asleep. Dasan was too young . . . it must have been Vasanti. But so unlike his sister to do such a thing!

He did not dare to waken anyone now. He would have to wait until morning. Vasanti!

He must get the money back. He fought against the sting of tears that crowded into his eyes. He must find the money.

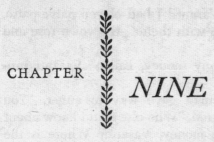

CHAPTER

NINE

When he awoke next morning, Raman lay looking up at the rough beams above his head. For a moment he felt nothing. Then with a sick wave it came flooding back: his money!

He sat up, throwing aside his blanket. Quickly he pulled out the loose brick and knelt down to peer into the hole, to make sure once and for all that the money was not there. The hollow was empty.

Vasanti! He straightened up and looked toward his sister's place on the floor. She was just stirring. "Vasanti!" Raman's voice was low and tense. "Vasanti, where is it? What did you do with it?"

Vasanti stared at him, her dark eyes wide with the effort of awakening.

"The money, Vasanti! I had eleven naiye-paise. What did you do with them?" His voice rose and broke.

"I didn't see any money, Enna," Vasanti protested.

Desperate, Raman gave way to anger. "You must have!" he cried. "Who else could know about it? Where is the money, Vasanti? Where is the money?" He was beside her, shaking her. Vasanti began to cry. Dasan, awakened from sleep, joined in, frightened.

"Raman." It was his mother's voice from the doorway. "Vasanti did not take your money. Let her go."

Raman sat back on his heels, his arms dropped to his sides. His mother gestured to the two younger children to leave. Vasanti scrambled up, pulling Dasan by the hand, and stumbled to the door, wiping the tears from her cheeks with the back of her hand.

"But, Amma, she must have taken it," Raman protested when they were gone. "Who else could have?"

"She did not take it," Raman's mother said quietly. "I did."

Raman stared. "Amma!" He ran his tongue

around his lips, to moisten them. "Amma, that was my money from what I earned! Appa said I could keep it, to buy books."

"I took it yesterday morning," his mother went on, her voice still quiet. "You were not at home, or I would have asked you. There was not enough money in the house to buy rice. I had to take it. Last night I would have told you, but you were so excited over the Merkin lady and her flowers, I thought I would wait and tell you this morning."

"But it was mine!" Raman protested, scarcely hearing all that his mother said. "It was mine! To buy books!"

"To buy books!" His mother's voice was rising now. "You would buy books when we have not enough food! You would fill your head with stories of heroes and battles that happened long ago, while now, right now, we have barely enough to eat. From day to day we are not sure of having money to buy rice for the next meal. Books! Books! Which do we need, tell me: books or food?" He had never seen her like this. Horrified, he watched the tears swell up into her eyes. His mother crying! She who never cried!

Anger left him. "Amma, please!" She was squatting on the floor now, her sari drawn up to cover her face. He must comfort her. "Amma, it is nothing. The books —" he swallowed hard "— the books do not matter. It was my fault. I did not bring enough money that day when I first tried to find flowers. It will be different now. Please, Amma. I will earn more."

His mother lifted her head at last. The tears were gone. Her smooth dark cheeks showed no sign of them. "You will have your money back, Raman, as soon as the money comes from your father. And now let us talk no more of it. There is much work to be done."

Raman rose slowly, numbly. "I'll go and come, Amma." He stepped outside the house.

Vasanti and Dasan, their fright forgotten, were playing now down by the stream, splashing each other with cold water and squealing. Raman looked at them, scarcely seeing them, sick with the sudden glimpse into the fear that lay hidden in his mother's heart. What was it his father had said, that morning at the bus stand? "I have talked with your mother . . . she perhaps does not understand quite so well that it is important to dream . . ."

"Appa was wrong," Raman thought heavily. "It is not that she does not understand. It is only that she is afraid. It is fear that keeps her face drawn

105

tight and keeps the smile from her lips. Fear, and not anger. She is afraid we will not have money, afraid we will not have rice."

Suddenly he was old, and the pity he felt toward his mother was the pity he would feel toward a small child. He felt hot tears rising. He choked back the tightness in his throat and looked off down the ravine to where Vasanti and Dasan were playing. How he envied them their laughter!

"They don't know," he thought. "They don't really know about things like money and rice. They feel hungry and they eat, and they don't know what it is to be afraid. They don't know. I wish I didn't know either."

Three more days passed. Then one afternoon as Raman walked up the bazaar street, Muttuswamy the bus driver hailed him.

"Eh, Thambi, I have something here for you!" Raman ran over to where Muttuswamy stood outside the bus office. The driver handed him a brown envelope. "Your father brought it to me just as the bus was leaving the city. He said to tell you all is well now and that he will send more as soon as he can."

Raman stammered acknowledgment and set out

up the bazaar hill at a running pace. He knew well enough what the envelope contained. There would be no more worry about rice now!

Raman's mother took the envelope he handed her, without speaking. She opened it and looked at the bills inside. Then she looked up at Raman. She took out one bill and handed it to him. "Go back to the bazaar, Raman, and bring a half measure of rice, and some vegetables and spices for a curry. You know what kind to get." Raman took the money and turned to go. "And, Raman —" he stopped, turning back "— when the shopkeeper gives you the change, count out sixteen naiye-paise and keep them for yourself."

"Sixteen, Amma? But —"

"I know. There were only eleven when . . . that day. But you have earned five rupees since then, and you have not been keeping your own naiye-paise out."

Her voice was quiet, almost expressionless. Raman stood silent, eyes downcast. She had noticed, then! The memory of that morning three days ago was painful still, that frightening glimpse into the fear that his mother concealed behind her outward calm. He looked up into his mother's face and saw that she was smiling.

"Go now, my son, it will be late." There was tenderness in her voice now. Feeling knotted Raman's throat. He could not think what to say.

He opened his mouth, but no words came. Clutching the bill in his fist, he turned and ran blindly out of the house, leaping up the embankment to the road without bothering to follow the path. At the top he paused. If only he could let his mother know how he felt!

He half turned back toward the house, and saw that his mother had come to stand in the doorway, looking after him. He waved, and saw her lift her hand in reply. She was still smiling.

On his way up the bazaar street once more, with the rice and vegetables and spices tied in a cloth and slung over his shoulder and the sixteen naiye-paise knotted in his shirttail, Raman stopped by the stall of Tumbuswamy the bookseller.

"Eh there, Thambi, have you come to buy your book already?" the old bookseller called when he caught sight of Raman.

"Not today, Tata, but soon." Raman stood on tiptoe to peer at the shelf where the little pile of booklets lay. "I have sixteen naiye-paise saved already," Raman boasted. "By next week I shall have enough for the book." The search for the hill flowers was going well. Each day he found four new plants to take to the Merkin lady; and the rupee he earned for the plants, plus any money made from selling pine cones or mushrooms or berries, meant at least one naiya-paisa a day and often some extra to be added to the next day's earnings, until a whole rupee was accumulated and another naiya-paisa earned. Now that he had the sixteen naiye-paise, it would not take long to save the amount needed for the book.

Raman tore his gaze away from trying to read the titles on the little paper booklets. He lifted the parcel of rice and vegetables to his shoulder and turned to go. It was then he saw the other book.

It was a real book, not a booklet bound in thin paper. Tumbuswamy had set it down in a corner of the glass case, down toward the front, in a shallow box lined with tissue paper. It was a thick book, bound in shiny black, and the tile on its cover gleamed in letters of gold. The cloth full of rice and vegetables slid from Raman's shoulder to the ground again as he stared.

"Tata." His voice was almost a whisper. "That book — what is it?"

"Ah, Thambi, that is a real book. Never in the years I have been here have I seen such a book. It is a real prize."

"Tata, could I — could I see it?"

"I cannot let you touch it, Thambi. But I'll take it out for you." Tumbuswamy carefully wiped his hands on a cloth and then opened the glass case with the little key that hung on a string around his neck. He reached in and lifted out the box with the book inside it. Gently, carefully, he brought it over to the low counter and laid it down where Raman could see it.

"The *Ramayana,*" Raman breathed softly, reading the golden letters across the front. The classic story of Rama, the great Indian hero for whom Raman himself was named. The story of the war between Rama and the demon king Ravana of the island Lanka, who had kidnaped Sita, Rama's beautiful queen.

"It has pictures also," Tumbuswamy was saying. His old hands trembled a little as he turned the pages of the book to one of the illustrations, a picture of Hanuman, the winged monkey, Son of the Wind, whose monkey army fought on the side of Rama against the demon king. Such colors! Brilliant red, golden yellow, green, blue. Raman had never seen a book with colored pictures in it. His own booklets had only rough pen drawings, the same color as the printing.

Raman watched in silence, not conscious that his

mouth hung open, as Tumbuswamy gently closed the book and replaced it in its box. Only when the book was back in its place in the glass case did he come to with a start. "Tata," he whispered, "I have never seen a book like that."

"Nor I," said Tumbuswamy. "It belonged to a very rich man, a scholar, who had it especially bound as you see it, with the letters all in gold."

"How — how much does it cost, Tata?"

"I am asking ten rupees, Thambi. But just between ourselves, I shall probably sell it for seven."

"Seven rupees!"

"Seven rupees," Tumbuswamy repeated. "Or, I might even let it go for six and a half rupees, but not a paisa less. At that it is a real bargain for a book like that." He took a cloth and began dusting off the top of the glass case.

"Tata," said Raman suddenly, "someday I am going to buy that book."

Tumbuswamy stopped his dusting to look at the boy before him. "Someday," he said, "perhaps you will."

"But it will take a long time," Raman went on, a catch in his voice, "maybe — maybe by then it won't be here."

"Maybe it won't," Tumbuswamy agreed, "but

maybe it will."

"I'll — I'll go and come, Tata," said Raman abruptly, and he lifted the cloth parcel to his shoulder once again, and turned and almost ran up the street away from Tumbuswamy's stall. It was possible to want something so much that the wanting of it could hurt. That was the way Raman felt about the book.

Six and a half rupees! Who could pay six and a half rupees for a book? But a book like that was a bargain at the price, so Tumbuswamy said, and Raman believed him. Why, with such a book Raman would be like a scholar himself. It was a book like those the Merkin lady had on the shelves of her bungalow. Who would ever think that such a book could be found in the little stall of Tumbuswamy the bookseller?

Six and a half rupees. One naiya-paisa for himself out of every rupee he earned. One hundred naiye-paise to make one rupee. Six hundred and fifty naiye-paise to make six and one half rupees. Six hundred and fifty rupees he would have to earn to have enough for the book!

Raman stopped short in the middle of the road. Six hundred and fifty rupees! And he had told Tumbuswamy that he would buy the book someday! How Tumbuswamy must have laughed to himself. Six hundred and fifty rupees!

But perhaps, Raman thought, going on more slowly, perhaps there is a way. Perhaps I will find a way to earn more money for myself. Somehow, someday I must have that book. Someday I will.

CHAPTER *TEN*

The days passed. The coins tied in the cloth and tucked behind the loose brick numbered thirty-eight now, but Raman did not think of buying one of Tumbuswamy's paper-covered books. True, he stopped by Tumbuswamy's stall each time he went to the bazaar. But he never glanced at the shelf where the little pile of books lay. He had eyes only for that gold-titled book that lay on its bed of tissue paper at the front of the glass case.

"Someday I am going to buy that book," Raman would say each time as he was ready to leave. Let Tumbuswamy laugh if he wished! But the old bookseller did not laugh. He only nodded his head and repeated his usual answer:

"Someday, Thambi, perhaps you will."

"But maybe it won't be here by then, Tata."

"Maybe it won't, Thambi, but maybe it will."

Things were going well now. Every week or so the bus driver brought a brown envelope for Raman to take home to his mother. To be sure, the money was not enough for all the things they needed, but at least they need no longer fear that there would not be rice to eat. The baby was warm in new winter clothes now, and another water vessel had replaced the old one that had been leaking for so long.

Raman did not gather pine cones any more, for there was almost no market for them anyway. Instead, he devoted his time to hunting flowers for the Merkin lady. As time went by it became harder and harder to find new kinds of flowers, and he had to go farther and farther beyond the lake to look for them. But sometimes the Merkin lady was particularly pleased when he found a flower that was rare, and then she would add extra coins to those she usually gave him. And one day, when he brought a lily plant that he had found growing halfway up a cliff, she gave him a whole rupee for that flower alone.

Whenever Raman had time, he stayed to watch the Merkin lady at her painting. It was fun to see how the deft strokes of the brush made the flower grow and bloom where once there had been only blank white paper. And the Merkin lady seemed happy to have him stay.

"You give me a chance to practice speaking Tamil," she told him one day.

"Amma speaks Tamil very well," Raman said shyly. It was true that sometimes the words the Merkin lady used seemed strange to his ears, and she spoke slowly, as though she were speaking in English, which was a slow language compared with Tamil. But Raman could always understand what she meant. It was not often that one heard the Merkin people speaking Tamil.

"Thank you, Raman. I think it is a very difficult language to learn. But in my school we must teach only in Tamil."

"Amma teaches school?" Surprised, Raman forgot to be shy. He could not picture the Merkin lady standing before a class with a pointing stick in her hand, like Munuswamy the schoolmaster.

"Yes, indeed." The Merkin lady seemed amused at his surprise. "We have a school down on the plains, a very big school — a college really, for older boys and girls."

"Girls!" Raman echoed, astonished. "You have girls in your college?"

"Certainly. Why not?"

"But girls do not need to read and write. They will just marry and keep house, and the learning will be wasted." The reasoning he had always accepted and repeated, parrot-like, from his elders sounded strangely hollow to his ears.

"Ah, there you have it!" the Merkin lady exclaimed. "But it will not be wasted. They will marry and keep house, it is true, but they will teach their children, and those children will teach their children, and so on. And then, too, Raman, in our school we teach many things besides reading and writing: how to farm, how to raise better crops, how to build better houses; and for the girls, how to prepare better meals, how to care for those who are ill . . . Then those who have learned in our school go back to their villages to teach others. That is the real importance of it all."

"Oh, Amma, if only I could go to a school like that someday!"

The Merkin lady's eyebrows lifted. "Who knows? Perhaps you will. How old are you, Raman?"

"Twelve — almost."

The Merkin lady nodded. "It will be quite some time before you are old enough, then. But in the meantime, if you work hard . . . tell me, do you go to school here?"

"Oh yes, Amma, I have been going for a year now — that is, I was going to school until my father went down to the plains. Even now I keep up with my reading, and when my father returns I shall start school again. Perhaps even before. I am anxious to go back. Already by the time I left I had caught up with the others my own age."

"You must have studied hard indeed to do so much in one year."

Raman nodded agreement. "I like the reading most of all," he went on, the words tumbling over themselves in his eagerness. "In my school I am the best in reading. And I am the first in my family to learn to read." He said this proudly, and paused to see whether the Merkin lady was impressed.

She was eying him thoughtfully. "That is a great responsibility."

Raman had already opened his mouth to say more, but he stopped and closed it instead, disappointed. He had expected her to say more than that, to show more admiration.

"I am going to be a great scholar someday," he continued after a moment. "I shall read many, many books. And I shall own the books myself. Shelves and shelves of them. I want to learn many, many things."

"Good," the Merkin lady nodded. "And then what?"

Again Raman stopped short, puzzled. He shifted feet a trifle uncomfortably.

"What will you do then, after you have learned many things?" the Merkin lady repeated. Her blue eyes searched his face keenly.

"Why . . . why then I shall know them, that's all," he answered, stammering a little.

For a moment he thought the Merkin lady was going to say something else, but instead she only nodded again and turned back to concentrate on her painting. Raman watched, first absently and then with closer attention, as with the skillful strokes of green and yellow and brown the flower began taking shape on the paper. With sudden courage Raman asked a question that had been in his mind for a long time.

"Why does Amma paint pictures of the flowers?"

For a while the Merkin lady was silent, intent

on her work, and Raman bit his tongue, regretting the question that it was surely not his place to ask. If he had angered her! . . . But then she glanced up with her usual smile. "I am going to make a book, Raman," she said, "a book with pictures of all the flowers that grow in these hills."

Make a book! Raman's eyes widened. To read a book was one thing — a fine thing, to be sure. But to write a book! Of course he knew that all the books he had ever seen — the paper-covered ones he owned, the books on the shelves in the Merkin lady's bungalow, the wonderful book in Tumbuswamy's glass case — all were written by someone. But here he was, face to face with a person who was actually writing a book. Someday these pictures he had watched grow on paper would be printed on shiny pages and bound in a book like those on the shelves inside the bungalow. And in a way he, Raman, had helped.

The thought was a pleasing one, but something else puzzled him. "Amma," he asked hesitantly, "why not paint the flowers from the garden? They are much more beautiful."

The Merkin lady put the final delicate touches on the painting, and then set down her brush and sat back in her wheelchair. She looked at Raman.

"Perhaps the garden flowers are more beautiful," she said slowly. "They are larger, more brightly colored. But they do not belong here. The hill flowers belong here, and so, even though many of them may not seem so beautiful, they are more important. I want people to know about them, and that is why I am writing a book about them.

"That is something you should remember, Raman," she went on, eyes on the painted flower now, yet seeming to look beyond it. "These things which belong here, which are a part of these hills, of this country — they are important, simply because they do belong. That is true not only of flowers but of many other things. Even of people. You belong here, Raman. I do not belong here, even though I have come many times to the hills, and spent many months in this bungalow, and many more in my school on the plains. Still I do not belong, and someday I shall be going away. When I teach the boys and girls in my school, I think of that. I am their teacher, and yet they are more important than I, for they belong here; and long after I have left they will still be here, to go on teaching others. You also, Raman," she turned to look directly at him, "you also belong here, in these hills, in this country; and so you too, like

121

the hill flowers, are important."

She leaned forward again suddenly and began to clear away the painting things from the table, putting the tubes of paint and the brushes away in the box again. Raman sprang to help. By now he knew exactly what needed to be done: the glass of water emptied, the board with its still-wet painting carried carefully into the bungalow and set on the shelf above the fireplace to dry, the table shoved back into its place on the veranda, the box of paints put away.

"Amma," Raman said when the work was done, "when the book is finished, do you think — could I see it?"

"Of course. But it will take a long time. I shall be leaving in three more weeks now, when my leg has healed enough, and that is not time enough to finish all the flowers. Next year when I come I shall paint some more. And the year after that, perhaps the book will be finished."

"I like books very much," Raman confided. "I save all the money I can to buy books to read." And the next moment, in a rush of excited words, he was telling the Merkin lady about the book in Tumbuswamy the bookseller's glass case, about the gold letters on its cover, the brightly colored illustrations, the wonderful stories it must have inside.

"Someday I shall buy that book," he boasted. "Someday it will be mine."

"It must be a very wonderful book."

"It is," said Raman. "It is a book that a real scholar would own."

The Merkin lady was studying him keenly. What was she thinking? She smiled then. "Good luck, Raman," she said gently. "Good luck. I hope someday you will have your book."

CHAPTER  *ELEVEN*

It was the last week of the Merkin lady's stay in the hills. Soon there would be no one for whom to hunt flowers, and there would not be a coin to add every day to the pile in the hiding place in the wall. Raman could go back to gathering pine cones with Vasanti, but so few, so very few of the bungalows were occupied that he would be lucky to sell two or three bags a week. There was no worry about rice, with the bus driver still bringing regularly the brown envelope from the city. But Raman's heart sank when he thought of the weeks ahead, when it might take days to earn a single rupee. He had fifty-seven naiye-paise now — more money than he had ever had in his life. But that was just a little over half of one rupee. And he needed six and a half rupees to buy the book!

One afternoon Raman sat alone outside the house, leaning against the wall and looking out over the vegetable garden that was now mostly dried, straggling stalks of plants. He picked up a thin twig and bent it in half, and then in half again and again until it was so small it would not bend any more, and then he broke each section off and tossed it into the air, watching as it fell back into the dust. Six and a half rupees, he thought. There must be some way to get six and a half rupees.

He did not hear Vasanti approach until she sat down beside him. "Uncle gave me some sweets, Enna. Do you want one?"

Raman shook his head. He wanted to be alone, to be able to think — think of some way to get six rupees more.

"You are so sad these days, Enna. Is it because you can't go to school?"

"No." He did not mean to sound so gruff. He saw the hurt in Vasanti's eyes and turned away from his own thoughts to look at his sister closely. He remembered suddenly the day they had gone hunting for mushrooms, just after their father had left. He remembered Vasanti's wistful voice saying, "You are lucky, Raman, to know how to read. I wish I could."

"Girls have no need for schooling." That was what he had said, and Vasanti had agreed. She too had heard it said so often! But now Raman thought of the Merkin lady, who not only read but could write books and teach school also; and of the Merkin lady's school, where girls as well as boys could learn — not just reading and writing, but many other things as well. Vasanti could scarcely hope to go to a school like that, but why should she not learn to read just the same?

And suddenly Raman heard his own voice saying, "Vasanti, would you like to learn to read?"

Vasanti stared, openmouthed.

"I said, would you like to learn to read? I'll teach you."

"Enna, do you mean it?" He saw the joy light her whole face.

"Of course, why else should I say it?"

"But girls —"

"There's no reason why girls shouldn't learn to read," Raman said firmly. "And I'll teach you. We'll start today itself."

Half an hour later Vasanti had finished her first

126

halting pages out of the old worn booklet from which Raman had first learned to read. Then their mother called Vasanti to bring twigs to start the fire, and Vasanti, her face still shining with pride, ran off down the slope to find them. Raman sat alone again. He was conscious of a strange, warm glow, unlike anything he had ever felt before. It was like having a power, he thought. A power to give knowledge to someone. A power to teach.

"I could teach Dasan, too," he thought. And then another thought crept in, unbidden: "I won't be the only one who knows how to read any more. "It gave him a somewhat empty feeling. It had been fun to think, to say, "I am the only one, the first one in my family and in my village who has learned to read."

"But this is better," he decided. "This feels even better." Still conscious of that warmth within, he stood up and started slowly down the slope to help Vasanti gather sticks for the fire.

The Merkin lady would be leaving on Friday, so she told Raman the next day. Raman nodded glumly. Friday was the day after tomorrow.

"Anyway," she went on lightly, "I am really beginning to wonder whether there are many more hill flowers left for you to bring. Although," she added, "we have not yet found the kind I wanted most."

"What kind is that, Amma?"

"A very special kind. I think it grows only in the deep jungle forest. It is a very beautiful flower, like butterflies clinging to a stem. Pink or white, or sometimes yellow or purple. In English we call it an 'orchid.' I don't know your Tamil word for it."

"Orchid," Raman repeated, and shook his head. He had not the slightest idea which flower the Merkin lady meant.

"Perhaps I can sketch it for you. Bring me a pencil and a paper from my table, Raman." When Raman returned, she took the paper and quickly outlined on it a bunch of long slender leaves, and then a delicate stem from which hung a number of dainty flowers, six-petaled, with one petal larger than the rest, flaring out and curling into a "lip" that stood out beyond the smaller petals. Raman could well imagine that from a distance those flowers would indeed look like butterflies on a stem.

"I have never seen anything like that here in the hills, Amma," Raman said at last, regretfully.

"What a shame. I would so much like to have

them, not only to paint but also to take down with me to the plains, to grow them in my house there."

"In these two days I shall look hard for them," Raman promised. "I may yet find them."

"I'll tell you what I shall do, Raman," the Merkin lady said slowly. "If you can find an orchid, I will give you three rupees for it. How is that?"

Raman stared, speechless. Three rupees! For one plant! And if he could find more than one kind . . .

"I will find them, Amma. I will find them." He hardly waited to give his usual farewell salute, but turned and raced up the drive. There was no time to lose. He had only what was left of today and all of tomorrow in which to find the orchids. The Merkin lady's bus would leave Friday morning, so he could not count on searching for the orchid on Friday at all. He must find out immediately where the orchid grew.

Whom could he ask? Munuswamy the schoolmaster? If he hurried, he might be able to reach the schoolhouse before the schoolmaster left. He turned down the road toward the bazaar, running until he could run no more, then walking as fast as he could while he caught his breath, then breaking into a run again.

Munuswamy the schoolmaster was just clicking shut the big padlock on the schoolhouse door. He looked up in amazement as Raman half slid, half ran down the little slope from the road, calling "Sir! Sir! Wait a moment, please!"

"Raman! What is it? Wait, get your breath first. Now then, are you coming back to school?"

Raman shook his head, still gasping. "No, not that. Not for a while anyway. It was only — I wanted to see you before you left — I was afraid you would have gone, and you are the only one I could think of to ask —" His breath failed him again, and he gulped in more air. Munuswamy waited, ducking his head to peer through the upper part of his glasses. "Sir," Raman went on at last, "I must find out about a flower that in English is called the orchid. Do you know about it?"

"Orchid?" Munuswamy the schoolmaster frowned. Raman waited tensely, holding his breath. "Orchid? No, I don't think I have ever heard the word. But then, the English I have learned does not include the names of flowers. Is it so important?"

"Oh, it is! I must find the flower, find where it grows."

"It grows around here then?"

"Somewhere in these hills."

"Well then," Munuswamy the schoolmaster said, a little sadly, "I am afraid I could not help you, even if I knew which flower you wanted. I am not from the hills, you know. My real home is on the plains. I do not know your hills that well — not even as well as you do, I'm sure. I'm sorry," he added, seeing Raman's disappointment. "I wish I could help you. I hope you'll find someone who does know."

Raman nodded glumly. "Thank you, sir." He saluted and left, making his way up the slope and along the road with steps that were slow and dragging now.

Who else might know? It would have to be someone who knew the names of flowers — his uncle, of course! Why hadn't he thought of it sooner? His uncle would be the one to ask, for he had worked in the gardens of the Merkin bungalows, and he knew the English names of many flowers. Surely he would know about the flower the Merkins called the orchid. Raman's steps quickened and his hopes rose.

It was time for the evening meal when Raman reached his house. He was so restless that he could scarcely eat. As soon as he could slip away, he set off up the path to his uncle's house.

"Well, Raman, this is a surprise. I have scarcely seen you these days. Your mother tells me you are off hunting flowers all day long. A pleasant pastime!" His uncle's voice had the familiar teasing edge to it.

"It is pleasant," Raman agreed, "but it is work also. Sometimes it is not easy to find them. I have to bring new kinds each time."

"I can't imagine why anyone would want to bother with wild flowers, with a garden full of flowers right outside the door. But then —"

"It is about flowers that I came to see you," Raman explained quickly, anxious to get the information he sought. "You know so much about flowers and their English names. Perhaps you can help me."

"Ah, is it the name of a flower you wish to know? Describe it to me — its color, shape. If it grows in the garden of the Merkin bungalows I will know it, for did I not spend many years in those same gardens? —"

"I know the name already," Raman broke in. If his uncle once started talking of his years as a gardener! "It is called in English the orchid."

"Orchid?" his uncle repeated. "Orchid? Are you

sure? Perhaps you have confused the name."

"I am sure of the name," Raman said. "It is not a garden flower, actually, but a hill flower. And it looks like butterflies on a stem."

"Butterflies on a stem!" his uncle echoed blankly. He shook his head. "I know many English names of flowers," he said. "If you wanted to know about larkspurs or foxgloves or marigolds or even chrysanthemums, I could tell you. But I have never heard of the orchid. I have never seen a flower that looked like butterflies on a stem."

CHAPTER  *TWELVE*

Raman walked slowly away from his uncle's house. His shoulders sagged with disappointment, and he felt tears pricking close behind his eyes. Who else could possibly know about the orchid?

It was early evening still. The sky was black with swollen clouds, and the rain would begin before long. Up on the slope above him he saw the flickering light of Tata Natesan's fire. He paused, one foot in midair. Tata Natesan! Perhaps — but no, he would not even know what the name "orchid" meant. Still, he might know of a flower that looked like butterflies, even if he did not know the English name.

Raman turned away from the path that led to

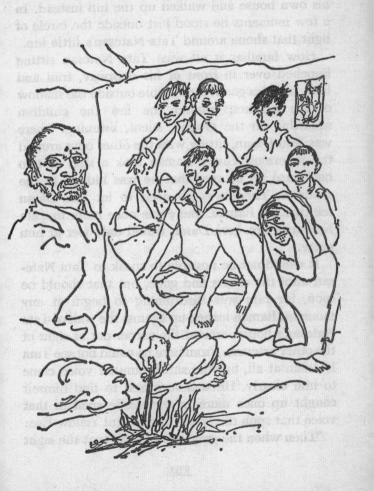

his own house and walked up the hill instead. In a few moments he stood just outside the circle of light that shone around Tata Natesan's little fire.

How familiar it all was! Tata Natesan sitting hunched over in front of his doorway, frail and bent, only his gaunt face visible outside the shadow of his blanket; around the fire the children squatting on the ground, silent, listening. There was Jesu-Dasan, sitting with the other boys around the innermost circle. Raman took a step or two backward, to be sure that he was hidden in the shadows. There was no need to let Jesu-Dasan see that he, Raman, had come once more to Tata Natesan's fire. Jesu-Dasan would only jeer at him anew.

It would not be possible to speak to Tata Natesan until the others had gone, but that should be soon, for rain was threatening to begin at any moment. Raman leaned up against the wall of Tata Natesan's house, around the corner out of sight of the other listeners. From here he could not see Tata Natesan at all, but the shrill, familiar voice came to him clearly. He was surprised to find himself caught up once more in the magic spell of that voice that spun the tale of the fearful Yellow Eye:

"Then when the great tiger found that the sight

of his eye was gone, he was filled with rage against all men. And he vowed that he would strike against any who dared to come to the slopes of his mountain. Night after night he prowled the slopes looking for the man who had blinded him. He could not hunt the wild animals as easily as he had done before, for when he sprang his sight deceived him and his leap would miss his prey, and before he could gather himself to spring again the animal would have fled to safety. Yellow Eye grew thin from lack of food, and his bones lay sharp beneath his striped hide. He was forced to go down to the outlying villages to find young animals, and that was dangerous, because then the hunters would track him down.

"But as time went by Yellow Eye began to learn to use his one eye with more sureness. Still, though he no longer went hungry, his anger toward mankind did not lessen. To this day he roams the slopes of the Bearded One, and all who go there must beware. In his fury he will attack anyone who dares invade his kingdom. He will take revenge for the loss of his eye."

There was silence when Tata Natesan's voice had ceased. The fire hissed and spat, and at the same time Raman felt a cold drop of water on his face.

Tata Natesan squinted up at the sky. "The rain has started," he said, and there were cries of disappointment from the children, for the storytelling had just begun. But Tata Natesan felt for his heavy walking stick and scattered the fire with the end of it. Then he drew his blanket closer about him with one hand, and holding his stick with the other he tried to lift his thin, bent body from the ground. Forgetting his desire to remain unseen, Raman sprang forward to help him. How light he was!

When he was on his feet, Tata Natesan turned to peer at Raman. "Who is that? You, Selvam?"

"I am Raman," the boy answered. "Selvam is my father." Tata Natesan stood looking at him, as though still seeing the boy Selvam who had come so many years before to hear stories in the firelight.

"Tata Natesan," Raman said quickly, "you know everything about the hills. Do you know where I can find the orchid? Surely you must have seen it?"

"Orchid?" Tata Natesan repeated. "Orchid? Is it an animal?"

"No, no!" cried Raman, impatiently. "A flower! A flower that looks like butterflies, pink or yellow or white, butterflies clinging to a stem. It has long, thin leaves, and it grows somewhere in the jungle forest."

"Butterflies," Tata Natesan echoed. "Butterflies! Ah, yes — I think I know. In the jungle forest, in the trees that line the ravines of the Bearded One, that is where it grows."

The Bearded One! The fearful mountain that was Yellow Eye's domain!

"Tata Natesan, are you sure? Isn't there some other place to find it?"

A warning rumble of thunder rolled over the hills. Tata Natesan shook his head. "On the slopes of the Bearded One, in the ravines. That is where it grows, Selvam." He turned to go into his house. A flash of lightning showed his scant white hair, his carved cheeks, the dark hollows that were his eyes. As the door closed behind him, Raman heard his high, thin voice once more: "Butterflies, Selvam . . . on the slopes of the Bearded One."

Raman turned back across the little clearing where the fire had been and found himself face to face with Jesu-Dasan.

The other boy was staring at him, eyes narrowed. Raman clenched his fists at his sides, steeling himself for the taunts that were sure to come. Head high, he walked across the clearing toward the path that led to his own house. But there was only silence, and as Raman came nearer, Jesu-Dasan turned and stalked off into the darkness.

Raman hurried on down the hill toward his own cottage. He could not see in the darkness, but his bare feet felt their way along surely, over the wet grass of the slope, the chill, hard ground of the gully, the broken earth of the cultivated space that surrounded his house. Rain thudded on his face and arms as he ran, and lightning forked through the sky beyond the hill in the direction of the lake. As he slipped in through the door, the monsoon downpour began in earnest.

Dasan and Vasanti were sound asleep, huddled together under the mended blanket. As Raman slipped past them he heard his mother's low voice. "Raman?"

"Yes, Amma."

"You must be wet with the rain. Wrap yourself well in your blanket."

"I will, Amma." Raman groped his way to his own corner, found his blanket, and drew it around his shoulders. Then he made his way carefully through the darkness to his mother's side.

"Amma."

"Yes, my son."

"Tomorrow I want to go very early, before the sun is up. The Merkin lady wants some special flowers, and I will have to go far to find them."

"Where do they grow?"

Raman hesitated. Then he said slowly, "I am not sure, but Tata Natesan thinks they grow in the jungle forest, over in the direction of the Bearded One." He did not say "on the slopes of the Bearded One," for he knew the thought that would leap to his mother's mind.

"There is no danger, Amma," he assured her hastily, before she could protest. "I will mark my path clearly, and if I do not find the flowers by noontime I will turn and come back, so that I will be home before sunset. And anyway," he added, knowing full well what must be in her thoughts, "Yellow Eye is just a story. Munuswamy the schoolmaster says so. No tiger could live as long as he is supposed to have lived, and especially not a tiger with one eye. It has been many, many years since any tiger has actually been seen in this part of the hills." He meant his voice to sound brave and sure, but hearing it, he wondered. "The Merkin lady will pay me well," he went on quickly. "If I find the flower, she will give me three rupees."

"Three rupees!" His mother was silent a moment. "I do not like it," she said then. "It is too far for you to go."

"There is no danger," Raman insisted. "It will be daylight. Amma, do not be frightened by an old man's tales. Munuswamy the schoolmaster knows more, much more, and he says Yellow Eye does not exist. There is nothing to fear."

"I do not like it," his mother repeated, but Raman caught the uncertainty in her voice.

"I am sure Appa would give his permission," he went on quickly. "He himself said that Munuswamy the schoolmaster was probably right." Immediately he wished he had left that word "probably" out. It made the argument less convincing. But still, that was what his father had said, "probably." "I saw a group of men last season who had climbed all the way to the top of the Bearded One," he added as a final point. "They even spent the night up on the slopes. Could they have done that if the story of Yellow Eye were true?"

"Very well," his mother said at last. "Look in the far corner of the room, and you will find some rice wrapped in a banana leaf. Take it with you when you go. I will make fresh rice for our morning meal. But remember your promise, to start home by noon even if you have not found the flowers. Only then will I not worry."

"I'll remember. Good night, Amma."

Raman groped his way back to his own corner, spread his palm mat, and lay down. But sleep did not come. He could feel, almost hear, his heart pounding above the steady drumming of the rain on the roof. In the chilly darkness his thoughts whirled about him until it seemed to him that he could see the dizzy pattern they made in the blackness above his head.

Tomorrow he would go to the slopes of the Bearded One, to the kingdom of the dreaded Yellow Eye. But Yellow Eye was just a story, so there was nothing to fear . . . Only suppose Munuswamy the schoolmaster should be wrong? Suppose Yellow Eye did roam the mountain slopes seeking revenge for his blinded eye? "Munuswamy the schoolmaster can't be wrong," Raman told himself. "Munuswamy the schoolmaster knows. He did not know where the orchids were to be found because he is not from these hills. But he knows that Yellow Eye is just a legend because — well, because it is a story that just couldn't be true, that's all. And Appa says so too. He says Munuswamy the schoolmaster is right — 'probably right!'"

Raman was not afraid of losing his way. True,

he had never been in the direction of the towering mountain, but he knew how to find his way and how to mark it so that he could return by the same route. On that score there was nothing to worry about.

No, it was not the fear of losing his way that kept the sleep from his eyes. It was the remembered echo of Tata Natesan's voice: ". . . To this day Yellow Eye still roams the slopes of the Bearded One, and all who go there must beware . . . the slopes of the Bearded One . . . butterflies . . . on the slopes of the Bearded One . . ."

"I am not going to be frightened by an old man's tales," Raman whispered aloud in the darkness "I have not believed those tales since — since before I went to school. I am not going to be afraid."

To take his mind from the picture of Yellow Eye, he began to think about the book in Tumbuswamy the bookseller's glass case and about the stories that awaited him beneath that goldtitled cover. At last he felt his eyes become weighted with sleep. He rolled over, out of reach of a little trickle of water that had found its way down through the roof, and drew his blanket still closer about him. Moments later he was asleep.

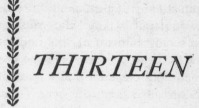

CHAPTER *THIRTEEN*

The rain had stopped. Through the small vent in the wall up near the roof Raman could see a sky turned the soft gray of a bulbul's wing, losing the blackness of night yet not ready to catch the light of dawn. Swiftly Raman slipped out from his blanket, shivering in the cold dampness of the room. His bare feet made no sound on the earthen floor. He groped his way to the corner and found the leaf-wrapped packet of rice. Then he crept along the wall toward the doorway.

Vasanti stirred as he passed and tried to pull her blanket closer around her. But her foot was sticking out through the hole which had come unmended again, and one corner of the blanket lay under Dasan, so that she could not pull it free. Raman stood still a moment, until he was sure that she would not waken. She would only ask questions, seeing him up at this hour, and he had no desire to answer them. Then he crept back to his own corner, picked up his blanket and, coming back, spread it carefully over Vasanti and Dasan, tucking it gently around Vasanti's bare foot. This done, he swiftly reached the door, slid the bolt back, and slipped outside.

His basket with the trowel inside it lay against the wall of the house. He slung the rope that held the basket over his shoulder, and put the packet of rice inside the basket as well. Then he scrambled up the steep bank to the road.

The morning was cold and wet, but the gray sky was clear of clouds and already flushed with orange over in the direction of the eastern slopes. Raman thrust his lower lip out so that his breath blew upward, and the warm steam from it touched his nose and his cold cheeks. He walked quickly — partly because he was in a hurry anyway, partly to keep his feet from aching with the wet coldness of the road. He followed the road that led downward to join the level drive on the bank of the lake. Great drops of water slid off the pointed ends of the blue gum leaves above his head and splashed onto the pavement below.

The lake water was dark and still, with wisps of mist trailing upward from among the water reeds. Even the frogs no longer trilled, and the water-lily buds were tightly clenched fists that would open only with the touch of the sun. A hoopoe bird, his long black-and-white crest folded back close to his head, was probing the wet lakeside grass with his sickle-shaped bill in search of grubs. He flew up in alarm as Raman passed, wings flashing black and white against his earth-red body, and settled on a stump not far away, crest fanned out now in his excitement, bobbing and calling out his strangely hollow cry: "Hoo-poo-poo! Hoo-poo-poo!"

By now Raman was not the only one about. Along the road came the fagot venders, bound for the bazaar with their loads of sticks balanced on their heads. A dhobi, or washerman, plodded along beside the donkey that carried the pile of clothes to be washed in the stream that flowed down from the lake. And there came Suppan the sweet-seller, pushing before him the little glass-walled cart that he would set up on the corner above the bazaar, where he would cook fresh hot *bondas* or *oopuma* — spiced wheat meal — over the little kerosene burner on the lowest shelf of the cart, or sell squares of sticky-sweet *Mysore-pak,* or *athirasam,* made from rice flour and thick brown-sugar syrup.

"Eh, Raman, you are up early today!" called Suppan.

"I'm going hunting," Raman answered. He did not say what he was hunting, and Suppan did not ask, for he thought it all a great joke.

"Well, a mighty hunter like you will need food to give strength," he jested. "Here, I have some *bondas* left from yesterday. They are still good, even if they aren't hot. Take them with you on your hunting trip." He set down the handles of the cart long enough to take the *bondas* out and wrap them in banana leaves, adding at the last minute two squares of *Mysore-pak* also. He handed them to Raman.

"Thank you, Enna." Raman put the leaf-wrapped packet in his basket.

"It is nothing. Good luck with your hunting! Bring back an elephant!" Suppan laughed heartily at his own joke, and trundled off down the road with his cart.

Raman took the *bondas* out and ate them as he walked. They were made of potato mashed and mixed with chopped chilies and onion and fresh

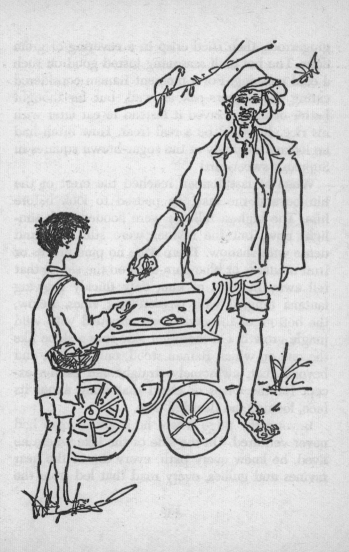

gingerroot, then fried crisp in a covering of gram flour. The hot chili seasoning tasted good on such a cold morning. For a moment Raman considered eating the *Mysore-pak* as well, but he thought better of it, and saved it instead to eat later with his rice. It would be a real treat. How often had he looked longingly at the sugar-brown squares in Suppan's sweet-cart!

When at last Raman reached the crest of the hill beyond the lake, he paused to look before him. The highest hilltops were flooded with sunlight now, but the ravines were still dark and dense with shadow. There were no pine groves or fruit orchards or blue gum trees on the slopes that fell away in front of him, only thickly growing lantana tangled with passion-fruit vines. Below, the bottom of the ravine was crowded with wild jungle growth. On the other side rose a slope like the one on which Raman stood, only higher, and beyond that, awesomely straight and barren except for the wisps of cloud that hung about its face, loomed the Bearded One.

Beyond the ridge where he stood, Raman had never ventured. On the side of the lake where he lived, he knew every path, every dip of the near ravines and gullies, every road that led from the town to the outlying farm settlements. He had gone many, many miles on paths he had known from the time he was old enough to leave the house alone. But here, on this side, there were no paths at all. Here, under the forbidding shadow of the Bearded One, hardly anyone ever came. But here grew the orchids, so Tata Natesan said.

In the light of morning, the story of Yellow Eye seemed foolish indeed. The slopes and the ravine beneath Raman were peaceful enough, full of the lighthearted chatter of bulbuls breakfasting on the lantana berries.

"If I go straight down from here," Raman decided, "until I reach the bottom of the gorge, and then walk up the gorge in the direction of the Bearded One, I'll be sure not to lose my way. I can mark the place where I came down the slope, and then I have only to return to the same spot along the bottom of the ravine and come back up the slope again."

It seemed easy enough. The ravine was not wide down below, and there was no danger of confusing the direction in which he walked. He noticed that, at the point where he stood, the ravine ran almost north and south, but that farther on it curved toward the east, toward the Bearded One.

He began his descent. It was not easy. He had to break through the rough lantana bushes with his body, and the ground underneath, still damp from the rain, was sometimes slippery and sometimes rough with pebbles that rolled away under his feet. The basket hampered his progress, for unless he held it with one hand it bumped against his body or caught on branches that jutted out. The passion-fruit vines seemed to reach out to wrap themselves around his arms and legs. He picked two or three ripe, wrinkled-brown fruits from the vines, and some wild berries also, to add to the store of food in his basket.

For a while it seemed to Raman that he was making hardly any progress at all. The depths of the ravine that he could see by peering over the shrubs around him seemed as remote as ever. But gradually he found the scrubby lantana of the upper slope giving way to unknown wild plants that became taller and taller until they reached above his head. Here, in an open stretch, coarse ferns brushed wetly against his legs. The bulbuls' songs that filled the air on the upper slope faded into the distance. From far away there sounded the ringing call of the barbet: "Too-KOOR, too-KOOR, too-KOOR." Another barbet answered from a low tree just in front of Raman, and he glimpsed a brilliant flash of green as the bird hopped from branch to branch, balancing its heavy body with its short, stubby tail.

He had almost reached the bottom of the ravine. He stopped to rest, letting the basket slide off his shoulder onto the ground and rubbing the sore place where the rope that held the basket had chafed his skin. How quiet the jungle forest was! He was used to the noise and activity of the town: bullock carts and Tamil voices, the slap of clothes being washed on the rocks, the clang of the bus gong, and the barking of dogs and squawking of chickens in the streets. Here there was silence, except for the high cries of the birds that receded more and more into the distance as he descended. Even the shadows were motionless, for the wind that blew on the upper slopes did not penetrate the thick growth in the ravine.

Raman started on again, walking more slowly now, scanning the ground as he went. He was entering the ravine forest, where full-sized trees, hung with woody jungle vines, crowded the bottom of the gorge. Anywhere along here the orchid might be growing. A shaft of sunlight struck through the trees and touched the pale striped hood of a cobra flower, making it glow as though with its own light. Around the trunk of a gnarled tree white wood violets traced a delicate circle. But nowhere did he see the pink or white "butterflies on a stem."

For a moment Raman thought he heard the wind rustling the leaves of the trees, but the air was still. No, it was the sound of water — a small, clear stream that tumbled through the tangled jungle growth on the floor of the ravine. He came to the water's edge and knelt on a large rock to drink from the cold pool beside it. The rock would serve as a landmark when he returned, he decided. He could recognize it easily: broad and flat, and green with moss, and with a curious hollow in the center that held water left from the rain. But just to make sure, Raman hunted around until he found a small pointed stone and with it scratched a mark across the mossy face of the rock. Now there would be no chance of mistaking it. He would walk upstream from here, and on his return he would simply follow along the stream to this point and then start up the slope again.

Raman could not rest long. His eagerness to find the orchid, now that he had reached the jungle forest, pulled him onward. He got up and began to walk slowly along the stream bank, sometimes stepping into the cold water when the bank was so overgrown that he could not pass. Always he scanned the ground carefully for a sign of the orchid. Except for the pad of his footsteps and the sliding rush of the water, there was no sound around him. Only, far away up the slopes, the barbet's call and its answer. He had the eerie feeling that perhaps the silence was due to his presence, that before he came and after he had left this shadowed world might be alive with the rustlings and voices of small creatures. For a time he made an extra effort to walk noiselessly, so that perhaps he might surprise some sign of life in the stillness. But there was none.

How long would it take to find the orchid? The sun was already high in the sky, peering down into the ravine and making strange, moving patterns on earth and water as it filtered through the foliage overhead. From its position Raman judged that he had already passed the point where the ravine turned eastward, and that now as he walked he was headed directly toward the Bearded One. At noontime, when the sun was at its height, he must start back, with or without the orchid. He had promised to do so, and anyway, he admitted to himself, he would not like to be on these slopes after dusk — Yellow Eye or no Yellow Eye.

"I must find the orchid," he whispered to himself. "I must find it." A secret thought pressed into his mind before he could shut it out. Suppose Tata Natesan were wrong? Suppose the orchid grew, not on the slopes of the Bearded One, but in some other part of the hills? Suppose Tata Natesan didn't really know what the orchid was. Then this, the only day Raman had in which to search for the orchid, would have been wasted. Tomorrow was Friday, the day the Merkin lady would leave for the plains. His chance would be gone.

I should not have gone to Tata Natesan, Raman thought with rising resentment. Perhaps it is true that he has lived so long with his stories that he knows nothing else. He did not even recognize me; he called me by my father's name. Perhaps he has talked so often of Yellow Eye and the Bearded One that he can think of nothing else. Perhaps that is why he told me the orchids grew here . . . But there was no one else to ask. Munuswamy the schoolmaster didn't know, nor my uncle. This was my only chance —

A sudden sound made him pause in the middle of a step. What was that?

He had grown accustomed to the silence around him. Now the silence seemed to shriek with the echo of that sound, though it must have been little more than the snapping of a twig.

He turned to look back the way he had come, but he saw nothing. There was only the dark stream gliding over the rocks, the tangled mass of vine and bush on either side of it, the gnarled trees overhead. There was not even a trace of the way he had come. It was as though the undergrowth had closed together again over the trail he had made as he pushed his way through it. He turned forward, took another step, and stopped once more.

There it was! This time he was not mistaken. There was a sound breaking the silence that surrounded him — a sound of movement in the underbrush downstream. He took a few more steps and paused again, still listening.

Crack! Rustle! It was closer now. There was no doubt about it: an animal, a large animal, was moving through the jungle forest, following Raman's trail.

Yellow Eye!

CHAPTER  *FOURTEEN*

A knot of panic wrapped itself around Raman's heart. What should he do?

He began to run, but running was almost impossible in the thick undergrowth. He stumbled over rocks lying along the stream bank, and thorny branches reached out to scratch at his arms and tear his shirt. The basket bounced behind him as he ran, and then it caught on a jutting limb and held him. He slipped the rope off his shoulder and plunged on, leaving the basket hanging there. Up ahead there was a heavy-limbed tree that leaned out over the stream. If he could only reach it, he could climb it and perhaps hide himself in its thick foliage.

The sound was coming closer; it seemed to fill the whole ravine. Raman reached the tree and scrambled up to the first branch. Higher he climbed, and higher, until the branches above would no longer bear his weight, and then he clung, trembling, to the trunk of the tree and waited while the crashing came nearer and nearer.

Through the tangle of undergrowth a shape loomed, and with a final lunge broke through into the small clearing at the foot of the big tree.

It was a cow!

Raman stared. A cow, a stray cow from some hill village. He had climbed a tree to hide from a cow.

Laughter rose in him like a gigantic bubble. He laughed so hard that he had to grab hold of the trunk of the tree to keep from falling. Then abruptly he stopped laughing and stared in astonishment.

There, nestled in a crotch of the tree, almost within reach of him as he clung there, was a plant with long, slender leaves and with flowers that looked like pale pink butterflies clustered together on a slender stem.

The orchid!

Raman squeezed his eyes shut, hard, and then opened them wide and looked again, scarcely daring to believe it. He edged his way closer to the orchid and touched it gently with one hand, aware of a faint, sweet fragrance as he did so. How beautiful it was! Dawn pink, with the lowermost petal, the "lip," a darker rose tinged with purple. Of all the flowers he had found for the Merkin lady — indeed, of all the flowers he had seen in the hills or gardens — this was surely the loveliest of all.

Where was his basket? He had left it behind in his frightened race through the jungle. He scrambled down from the tree. The cow was nowhere in sight. It must have wandered off up the ravine. In his excitement Raman had not even noticed its departure.

The basket still hung by the rope that was caught on the outjutting limb. Raman lifted it off and took out the food and laid it on a rock. Then, carrying the basket with him, he climbed the tree again to the branch where the orchid was growing. Gently he used the trowel to loosen the orchid from the debris of dead leaves and twigs caught in the crotch of the tree. He transferred it to his basket, breathing deeply of its fragrance, and then laughed from sheer delight. He had found the orchid! Tata Natesan had known after all: "In the jungle forest, in the trees that line the ravines of the Bearded One —" These had been his very words, "in the trees." But who had ever heard of plants that grew in trees? Raman had thought that Tata Natesan was confusing words as well as names. Or possibly in his haste he had never really thought about it at all.

Were there perhaps other kinds of orchids growing nearby? His excitement mounting, Raman scrambled down and climbed another tree. There was, indeed, another small orchid plant, but it was pink like the one he already had. He looked around from his vantage point in the tree. There, in that tree across the stream — was it not a splash of yellow color against that high branch?

He climbed down and plunged into the stream, not even wincing at the coldness of the water, and was soon scrambling up the trunk of the tree on the other side. Yes, it was another orchid — one with yellow, purple-streaked petals and a "lip" of velvety purple with yellow spots.

For a long time after that Raman searched in vain for yet another kind of orchid. And then, just as he was about to give up the search — for the sun was directly overhead — he found the largest of all: an orchid with yellow-green petals streaked with red, the lowermost petal white, flushed with deep, velvety purple at its base.

Not one but three orchids for the Merkin lady! His basket would hold no more, even if he had the time to look for them. Gently he arranged the orchid plants in his basket, sprinkling over them water from the stream. The pink one, the first he had found, was still his favorite. Its coloring was so delicate, the petals so fragile-looking, and it was the only one that had a fragrance also.

Three orchids! And for each orchid, three rupees: nine rupees in all!

The sum was staggering. Raman sat back on his heels, staring at the basket. Nine rupees! He had told his mother he might earn three rupees. What would she say when she found that he had brought, not three rupees, but nine: six rupees extra!

A sudden thought clutched at him. Six rupees extra! Six rupees that his mother did not expect him to bring.

"I couldn't," he whispered aloud, before the thought had even fully formed.

"Yes, you could," another voice seemed to answer. "Why not?"

Why not give his mother the three rupees that

he had said he would earn if he found the orchid? She would have no way of knowing how much he had actually received. He could keep the remaining six rupees. Or rather, he could spend it — spend it for the book in Tumbuswamy the bookseller's glass case.

"I could have that book," he thought. "I could really have it for my own. I would own a real book, a scholar's book."

His mother would be pleased enough to have the three rupees, which was more than Raman had ever earned in a single day. As for the book — she would not even notice it, surely. He would be going off by himself to read it anyway; and when he was not reading it, it would be tucked away in his corner where no one would disturb it.

"It would not be right," Raman admitted. But then, was it right that he should have to give up his schooling to work every day while his father was gone? He had worked hard, too. He had spent hours gathering pine cones and hunting mushrooms, and even more time searching for flowers for the Merkin lady. Indeed, it had been his idea of selling flowers to make extra money that had led him to the Merkin lady's bungalow in the first place, and without the money he earned from the hill flowers things would have gone badly indeed. Now today he had walked farther than he had ever walked in his life, to find the orchids the Merkin lady was so anxious to have before she left. Had he not earned those extra rupees for himself?

Besides, Raman told himself, they no longer need fear that there would not be money for rice, for the money that his father sent from the plains was enough to feed them at least, if not for other things.

Raman knew then that the decision was made. Tomorrow the book would be his.

He got up and picked up his packet of rice and the fruit and *Mysore-pak*. Down by the edge of the stream he found a smooth rock on which he sat while he ate. The stream was alive with shadows of leaves and ringlets of sunshine that glanced off the flowing ripples and broke into streaks and splashes of gold. Here and there circles of light floated across the dark, mossy bottom of the stream, and slim, dark fish darted out and back again. When he had finished eating, Raman sat with his shoulders hunched and his arms hooked around his bent knees, feeling warm waves of excitement through him.

It would be too late when he returned to go buy the book today. But first thing in the morning he would slip away to the bazaar, and he would stride up to Tumbuswamy's little stall and say, "Tata, I have come to buy your book."

And Tumbuswamy would say, "Which one do you want, Thambi?" and reach for the little pile of paper-bound booklets on the shelf.

"Oh no, Tata," Raman would say, "it is *that* book I want." And he would point to it through the glass.

"You are joking, Thambi," Tumbuswamy would protest.

"Oh no, I am not joking." Raman would laugh out loud at the old bookseller's astonishment. "I have come to buy the book. Did I not tell you I am going to be a scholar? And did you not say that that is a scholar's book? And did I not promise to buy it for myself someday?"

Then Tumbuswamy would take the money from Raman's hands, and, still wondering, he would count the bills and the coins. He would take the book out of the glass case and dust it off gently with his cloth, and put it into Raman's hands.

"And then what?" Raman started, sure that the words had been spoken aloud. He glanced around uneasily, but he was alone as before.

"And then what?" That was what the Merkin lady had said, the day Raman had talked to her of the books he would read and the many things he would learn.

Well, after he had bought the book, then what? Why, then he would take the book and read it. And then? Raman shifted uneasily on the rock. It was as though someone were with him, probing his thoughts. Then the book would be his. It would be the first of many, many such books that he would own. A woodcutter's son need not be just a woodcutter. He could become a scholar if he chose!

Almost angrily Raman jumped up and strode back to where his basket sat in the shade of a tree trunk. He slung the rope that held the basket over his shoulder and set off downstream as fast as he could, thrusting his way through the underbrush, one arm around the basket and the other arm held up in front of his face to protect it. When he came to the big flat rock with the mark scratched on its mossy surface, he turned upward, up the steep slope. His hands were scratched and cut from grasping the rough stems of shrubs to pull himself upward, but he did not notice. His thoughts were on the book — the book that would now be his.

CHAPTER *FIFTEEN*

It was late afternoon when Raman reached the hilltop bungalow. He marched in through the gate and up the drive to the edge of the veranda. The Merkin lady was not in sight.

"Amma!" Raman called, forgetting all shyness in his excitement. "Amma!"

In a few moments the Merkin lady appeared, not in her wheelchair but walking with crutches, the plaster cast replaced by an ordinary bandage.

"Raman! I had given you up today." She was surprised and pleased.

"Just see, Amma," Raman said eagerly. "I've found the orchids. Not one kind, but three!"

"Is it true? Bring them and let me see." She was

as excited as he. She made her way over to a chair that stood on the veranda and let herself slowly down into it. Raman slipped the basket off his shoulder and carried it to her.

"You did find them!" she exclaimed. "Raman, these are beautiful. I never dreamed —" She forgot to speak in Tamil, but the tone of her voice needed no translation. Raman stood by, grinning, as she examined each orchid in turn, exclaiming over them, naming them with long, strange-sounding names, until at last she sat back and looked at him. "You have done a fine job, Raman," she said in Tamil. "I did not dare to hope for such good fortune. You have certainly earned your money. Wait here while I bring it."

Raman stood on one foot and then the other until at last the Merkin lady reappeared. He stepped forward, holding out his cupped hands as she counted the bills into them: "Two-four-six-seven-eight-nine. Nine rupees for three orchid plants." She smiled. "More than enough for your wonderful book, Raman."

Raman drew in his breath sharply. How had she guessed what he was going to do? But of course she could not know the whole story. She only remembered that one day he had told her about

the book he wanted so much — the book that cost
six and a half rupees. He nodded, not wanting to
speak.

"Well, good-by then, Raman. I am to leave on
the early bus tomorrow morning. It is not likely
that I will see you again. You have worked well,
and I hope I may see you here next year. I will be
able then to hunt flowers for myself, but I will need
a guide on the hill trails and someone to carry the
basket. And you shall show me your book, too."

"Good-by, Amma," Raman answered in a low
voice. "Many thanks." He touched his forehead
in a farewell salute, and turned and walked down
the drive for the last time.

Before he reached his house, Raman stopped
just off the road, in the shadows of a young pine
tree. He looked up and down the road. There was
no one in sight. He drew the wad of bills out of his
shirt, where he had thrust them, and counted out
the three one-rupee bills. Holding them in one
hand, he folded up the remaining six rupees and
tied them in a corner of his shirttail. Then he
tucked his shirttail into the waist of his shorts and
walked on, clutching the three rupees in his hand.

His mother was just setting out the banana
leaves for the evening meal. She looked up at his

approach, and he saw relief smooth away the worried lines that creased her forehead. "Raman, it is good you have come. Wash quickly; you must be very hungry."

"I found the orchid, Amma," Raman said. His voice sounded flat to his own ears. "Here — here are the three rupees." He held out the money.

"Well done, my son. I am proud of you." His mother's voice was warm, pleased. She must have worried about him, he thought, more than she would admit. Now the worry was replaced by pride, because he had been successful in his search.

"This will buy a warm jacket for Dasan," his mother was saying with satisfaction. "He has been catching chill so often. Tomorrow we will go to the bazaar — but Raman, you have not kept your own money, your three naiye-paise."

"It does not matter," Raman mumbled, feeling his cheeks grow hot. "Later, when there is change." He turned and hurried outside.

Vasanti was squatting outside the house, drawing with a stick in the dirt. She looked up at Raman, her small face aglow with pride. "Just see, Enna, I've been practicing. I was hoping you'd be home before it was too dark for a lesson." Her voice ended on a question, hopefully.

It was on the tip of Raman's tongue to brush her aside. He was tired and full of the day's excitement, and a strange restlessness possessed him. But he checked himself, seeing the hope in Vasanti's eyes, and spoke gently instead.

"After supper, Thangachi, we'll have our lesson. There should be light still. Come, let's go down to the stream and wash."

Vasanti jumped up, pleased that Raman had asked her to go with him. As they walked back, hands and arms and faces still tingling from the cold stream water, she ventured to speak again.

"Enna."

"Yes, Thangachi?"

"I was showing Mariamma how much reading I have learned." Mariamma was Vasanti's closest friend, and Jesu-Dasan's younger sister.

"Was she properly impressed?" Raman teased.

"Oh yes," Vasanti was quite serious. "She —" Vasanti hesitated. "She wants to learn too, Enna." The words tumbled together. "She wants so much to learn. Enna, do you think — could you teach her also?"

Raman frowned. He had not intended to become so involved in this business of teaching. It might take more time than he wanted to spend. He might not even have time for his own studying, for the reading he intended to do (from the book, from the *Ramayana*, a voice seemed to whisper, sending a thrill of anticipation through him). He could always put Vasanti and Dasan off if he did not feel like giving a lesson, but if there was someone else — still, as he thought about it, the idea pleased him. He remembered the heady sense of satisfaction he felt each time he finished a lesson with Vasanti, each time he saw the knowledge growing in her and knew that it was he who helped it to grow. And so at last he nodded in agreement. "All right. Tell Mariamma she can come."

"Oh, Enna, I'm so glad!" Vasanti gave a skip of delight. They had reached the house now. The rice was already served, white and steaming. Usually they ate in silence, but tonight was an exception. Raman told them of his adventures: of the encounter with the cow, and the finding of the orchid, and how the orchid plant grew in the trees instead of on the ground. He ended abruptly, conscious of the part of the story he did not want to tell: the finding of the other two orchids. But the others did not seem to notice that the story was cut short, and Vasanti and Dasan plied him with eager questions and exclaimed, round-eyed, over his bravery in venturing into the domain of the dread Yellow Eye.

After supper, Vasanti ran off to call Mariamma, for there was still a remnant of daylight, enough to read by. But Mariamma did not come alone. With her came Jesu-Dasan himself, swaggering a little as he always did, hands in his pockets, lips pursed slightly as though he were trying to whistle but could not.

The two boys exchanged awkward greetings, followed by an even more awkward silence. It was Jesu-Dasan who broke the silence at last.

"Mariamma says you are teaching Vasanti to read and that you are going to teach her, too," he said slowly.

"Yes," Raman answered, adding to soften the shortness of his reply, "and Dasan too, though he is young yet." He was puzzled by something in Jesu-Dasan's voice. How many times in the past months had he heard that voice calling after him, jeering, taunting: "Bookworm! The Scholarly One! Look, there goes the Scholar himself!" There was no taunting in Jesu-Dasan's voice now.

Jesu-Dasan planted his feet firmly on the ground, wide apart, put his hands on his hips and looked straight at Raman. "Will you teach me also,

Raman?" he demanded.

Astounded, Raman opened his mouth to reply, still hearing those taunting echoes that had stung him for so long. But he closed it again without speaking, hearing the pleading behind the rough tones of the other boy's voice.

"You have been lucky, Raman," Jesu-Dasan went on, huskily. His arms dropped to his sides. His gaze was fastened on a point somewhere beyond Raman's head. "In all the settlement you are the only one who goes to school. You are the only one who has had a chance to learn to read. I am not the only one who wants to learn from you. There are others: Sellam, Muttu, Lakshman —" He named the other boys in the settlement. "You need not think yourself better than the rest of us, just because you can read," Jesu-Dasan added, with a sudden return of his former belligerence.

"No, of course not," Raman said quickly. "I have been lucky, that's all."

"We can't go to school in the town," Jesu-Dasan went on. "But if you could teach us, Raman, in the evenings after our work is done, the way you teach Vasanti and Dasan —"

Raman was silent. "I wonder if I could," he thought. "It would not be easy. How would I go about teaching so many? I don't have enough books. But we could write on the ground, and read from that. Or maybe Munuswamy the schoolmaster could help me get some old reading books."

The thoughts came tumbling faster and faster. Raman felt excitement mounting within him. He could do it! He would do it! He would be — he smiled at the thought — he would be a teacher! Not a schoolmaster — not yet — but a teacher just the same!

"I will do it," he announced suddenly. "Tell the others to come tomorrow evening. We can study here, where the ground is level for writing and there is plenty of room for all of us. I do not have books for so many, but we will start by writing on the ground and reading from that. Be sure to come in time, so that we will have enough daylight for our lesson. And then," he added, "afterward we can all go to Tata Natesan's fire."

"We'll be here tomorrow," Jesu-Dasan promised. "I'll tell the others."

Raman watched him go back up the slope, climbing it in great leaps and bounds instead of following the winding path. He took a deep breath, shakily. It was as though a wound had healed. He was conscious of a sense of well-being such as he had not known for a long, long time.

He would go again to Tata Natesan's fire. And though the tale of Yellow Eye might indeed be nothing more than a legend, made alive by the magic of an old man's words, Raman knew he would no longer scoff at Tata Natesan's stories. True or not, they belonged to the hills, even as Raman did. And because they belonged they were important.

There was little light left, only time enough for a page or two of reading with Vasanti. Raman sat down between Vasanti and Dasan, while Mariamma peered over Vasanti's shoulder. Vasanti read well, and even little Dasan could sound out a few words, putting a small finger under each circle or dot or loop of the Tamil script.

Long after the lesson had ended, Raman sat outside with his knees drawn up under his chin, staring out into the darkness. He found himself wishing that he could tell the Merkin lady what he was going to do. She had not seemed greatly impressed that day when he had told her that he was the first in his family to learn to read. What was it she had said? "That is a great responsibility." Not a great accomplishment, or some such word, as he had expected she would say, but a great responsibility. He had thought it a strange thing to say, and he had been disappointed.

If she knew about the teaching she would be very happy, Raman thought, and wondered why he felt so sure of it, and why it seemed to be important that the Merkin lady should know and think well of him. He remembered how, on that same day, she had talked of her own school: "We teach many things, Raman — not only reading and writing, but how to farm, how to build better houses. . . . Then those who have learned in our school go back to their villages to teach others. That is the real importance of it all."

Was that not what he, Raman, was about to do? He had learned much already in his school, he would of course learn still more when he resumed his studies; and now he was going to teach others, too. Next year when the Merkin lady returned he would tell her about it, perhaps even show her his "class." And then she might say indeed, "That is a real accomplishment."

Raman stood up then and stretched, and went inside. He unrolled his palm mat and lay down, huddled in his blanket. He was tired. His whole body ached. But sleep did not come.

It was excitement, he thought. The excitement

of finding the orchids. Or perhaps the excitement of the plans for teaching and the return of his friendship with Jesu-Dasan. No, something more than that. Of course, the book. How could he have forgotten even for a moment? In a matter of hours now the wonderful book would be his.

He closed his eyes and waited until the picture formed itself clearly in his mind: the shiny black binding with its gleaming gold letters spelling out the title; the brilliantly colored drawings inside; the lines of Tamil script that related the unforgettable adventures of Rama in his fight against the demon king.

Wait until Appa sees it, he thought. How proud his father would be of his scholar-son! But — how to explain to his father the purchase of such an expensive book?

"He will not know how much it cost," Raman told himself. But the question bothered him.

Perhaps it would be necessary to keep the book hidden for a while. Well, not hidden exactly, but tucked away in his corner, underneath the little pile of paper-covered booklets, or rolled up in his palm mat, which no one else ever touched. Except of course when he was reading the book, and then he would go off by himself anyway, so as to be undisturbed. Surely when Appa did find out about it, he would rejoice that his son owned a real book, such as scholars owned. Had his father not said as much that day at the bus stand? "When I was your age I too dreamed of becoming more than a woodcutter . . . Keep your dream, Raman. Hold onto it with all your strength. . . ." Was that not what Raman was doing?

But then against his will the rest of his father's words came pushing into his thoughts: "Take care now — you are responsible for the others. In my absence you are head of the household and, for the time being, the chief wage earner. I leave everything with you."

Suddenly, without knowing quite why, Raman pulled the blanket up around his face, and his thin shoulders shook with sobs — great sobs that came without tears, until at last he slept.

CHAPTER *SIXTEEN*

Scarcely waiting to finish his morning meal, Raman set out the next morning for the bazaar. Knotted in his shirttail were the coins from his hiding place, and the three two-rupee bills the Merkin lady had given him for the extra orchids. He strode along, not looking to right or left, conscious of the lumpy weight of the money against his body as he walked. This was the day of which he had dreamed for so long. This was the day the book would be his.

He had pictured this day to himself so many times. Yet strangely enough there was no dizzy, singing excitement to lighten his step or to carry him as though in a winged chariot along the winding hill road. Perhaps it was because he still could not believe that this was real. Yes, surely that was it. It was all too much like just another dream.

He stopped beside the road. No one was in sight. He pulled out his shirttail and fumbled with the knot that held the money. Why did his fingers tremble so? There, the knot was open. He took out the three two-rupee bills and unfolded them, smoothing them open as well as he could with one hand. Seeing the six rupees, there in his hand, brought some reality to it all. He held the bills between his teeth while he tied the knot around the coins once more. Then, clutching the bills in one hand, he went on his way.

He entered the bazaar street and passed the bus stand. The early bus had left already. Raman realized that he had half hoped to see the Merkin lady, to tell her about the teaching he planned to do. But it did not matter, he decided. He would see her next year. Just now the book was the important thing.

Down below he could see the little tin roof of Tumbuswamy's stall, and, as he came closer, the open front of it, and Tumbuswamy inside, dusting off the glass case.

"How surprised he'll be," Raman thought. "He'll

never believe me!" He wanted to walk faster, but the road was so steep that each step he took jolted him inside. He began to go more slowly instead, so that his heart would not pound so much.

Now he had almost reached the shop. He could see Tumbuswamy squinting out at the street. In another moment the old bookseller would catch sight of him, and Raman would wave . . .

Then a strange thing happened. A grayness came over his eyes, so that Tumbuswamy and his book-stall were blotted out, and instead Raman saw his own house as he had seen it that morning, with his mother squatting in the corner, blowing on the fire for the morning meal, and the baby kicking on a palm mat by her side, and Vasanti and Dasan still asleep on the floor. He saw the torn blanket, and Vasanti's bare foot sticking out through the hole. He saw his mother turn to smile at him, her eyes still full of pride from the day before.

Raman stopped in front of Tumbuswamy's still. He looked up into the surprised, wrinkled face of the old bookseller. He held out the hand that clutched the six rupees, and he opened his mouth to say, "I have come to buy the book, Tata!" But the words did not come.

"I will go and come," Raman said then, and

turning he ran off down the street. Not many doors away there was a cloth shop open. He went in and stood looking up at the glass-doored shelves that lined the walls and the bright bolts of cloth behind the glass.

"Well, Thambi, what can I do for you?" asked the storekeeper.

"I want a blanket," said Raman, hearing his own voice as though from a distance. "A warm woolen blanket. Red."

The shopkeeper reached up to a high shelf behind him and took down a red blanket. "Here is a fine one, Thambi. It arrived from the city, not two days ago."

Raman fingered the wool, careful not to let his face show that he was pleased with it. That was one of the first rules of bargaining.

"How much is it?" he asked.

"Eight rupees."

Raman rubbed his hand again over the blanket, smoothing out the surface and feeling the texture of the wool against the palm of his hand. He took a deep breath. Then he looked straight at the shopkeeper and said boldly, "I'll give you five rupees for it."

The shopkeeper stared. "You're joking, Thambi.

Five rupees for this blanket? Feel the wool in it — see how soft, yet heavy, it is. Look at the color, made by the finest dye. Seven rupees, Thambi, and it is a bargain for you."

Raman shook his head. "Five rupees and fifty naiye-paise."

"Thambi, you do not know what you are saying," protested the shopkeeper. "At that price I would be losing money. Six and one half rupees. That is the lowest I can accept."

"And I can give five rupees and seventy-five naiye-paise," said Raman firmly. "That is my last offer."

"A compromise, then," countered the shopkeeper. "A compromise. Six rupees. Never in my life have I sold such a blanket for six rupees."

Raman hesitated. "Five rupees and ninety-one naiye-paise," he said then.

"Six rupees, Thambi. What are nine naiye-paise, after all?"

"To me they are important. Five rupees and ninety-one naiye-paise," Raman insisted.

The shopkeeper threw back his head and laughed. "You are a real bargainer, Thambi. Five rupees and ninety-one naiye-paise it is." Still chuckling, he took the blanket and wrapped it in a piece of brown paper, tying it with a string.

Raman handed him the three two-rupee bills and took back the change. Nine naiye-paise — one for each of the nine rupees earned from the orchids. He added them to the others that were tied in his shirttail. There were seventy-five naiye-paise altogether.

He picked up the package, then set it down again and with one finger poked a hole in the brown paper so that the red of the blanket showed through. Clutching the package to him, he stepped out into the street and started back up the hill.

As he walked, he made himself picture how Dasan and Vasanti would look when they saw the blanket, their eyes and mouths round with delight. He thought how proud his mother's face would be, and how, when his father returned, he would tell him the story of the blanket and the search for the orchids that had made the buying of the blanket possible. He pictured the way the blanket would look in his house, making the whole room seem warmer with its flame-red color. And some of the warmth of the blanket seemed to envelope him as he plodded slowly up the bazaar street.

He told himself that he would walk right past

Tumbuswamy's stall without a sideways glance. But of course he could not.

His feet led him there, seemingly of their own accord, until he stood, as he had stood so many times, in front of the glass case on Tumbuswamy's counter. A sudden sick feeling clutched at his stomach when he saw the book. How beautiful it was! How the golden letters on its cover gleamed and beckoned! "The *Ramayana*," he read, whispering, and the word had music in it. He held the paper-wrapped package a little tighter against him.

For a long, long moment Raman stood looking at the book. Then he looked up into the face of Tumbuswamy the bookseller and said, "It is a beautiful book, Tata." His voice was still a whisper.

Tumbuswamy the bookseller, who was old and wise, and whose eyes saw many things, looked down at Raman and at the paper-covered package in his arms. He saw the tear in the paper and the red wool of the blanket showing through. And because he had also seen the six rupees in Raman's hand before, Tumbuswamy the bookseller understood, and his old eyes, as they looked at Raman, seemed suddenly a little wet.

"Someday," Raman said softly, "someday, Tata,

187

I am going to buy that book."

"Someday you will," agreed Tumbuswamy the bookseller.

"But perhaps — perhaps by then it won't be there."

"It will be here," said Tumbuswamy the bookseller. "It will be here, Thambi. I promise."